THE WAGON ... WITH MONEY!

The bank robbers followed the wagons the rest of the night. Virgil could see three mounted guards—so they faced five armed men. He'd long ago picked out the ambush spot.

Virgil took up a position in the brush on the other side of the road so they would have the wagons and guards in a cross fire.

"Fire at the mounted men first," he told Joel. "You won't have time to reload, so make 'em count."

The wagons did not appear till late in the afternoon. Virgil levered the rifle and took his hat off. Then he waited. . . .

The last covered wagon was on the slope when Joel fired. The lead horseman was flung back and toppled as the horse bolted.

Virgil swore, sat up and fired rapidly at the other two horsemen behind the wagon. There was a heavy fusillade of shots—then it was still. The smoke cleared slowly and Virgil stood up. He shoved his hat back on and walked down the arroyo, the rifle over his shoulder. The men were dead all right.

Each wagon bed was covered with a tarpaulin. Virgil sliced the cords with his knife and pulled the 'paulin off. He looked at the five wooden crates. There was a toolbox under the wagon seat. He found a claw hammer and pried the lid up on one of the boxes. It was packed with greenbacks. So were the other boxes!

With shaking fingers he lit a cheroot and puffed, trying to calm his racing pulse.

He was rich as hell!

→◆→ WESLEY ELLIS ◆←

LONE STAR

AND THE
BANK ROBBERS

J

JOVE BOOKS, NEW YORK

LONE STAR AND THE BANK ROBBERS

A Jove Book/published by arrangement with
the author

PRINTING HISTORY
Jove edition/November 1990

ISBN: 0-515-10446-9

Jove Books are published by The Berkley Publishing Group,
200 Madison Avenue, New York, New York 10016. The name
"Jove" and the "J" logo are trademarks belonging
to Jove Publications, Inc.

PRINTED IN THE UNITED STATES OF AMERICA

10 9 8 7 6 5 4 3 2 1

★

Chapter 1

The bank officers of the Gunnison Bank met in the usual room, upstairs over the bank, on Wednesday afternoon. There was the bank owner and president, J. M. Thompson, and officers: Homer Tredwell, Jerome Gibbs and Harrison Edwards. They met without a recording secretary. If he felt it necessary, Thompson would make a few scratchy notes and put them away in an inside pocket of his black coat.

The room was not large and was paneled in pine that had been stained dark. There were no pictures on the walls, and the two windows were heavily draped so that it was necessary to light three lamps to see well. The coal oil made the room smelly.

One of the clerks from downstairs had brought in glasses and a pitcher of lemonade, which he placed in the center of the long table. He had also brought pencils and a small stack of paper in case anyone wished to write.

Thompson was a stout, white-haired man with a pompous air. He was fish-eyed and florid and looked every bit like a successful mortician. He was probably the wealthiest man in town and everyone bowed and scraped to him—which he dearly loved and expected.

Homer Tredwell had been good-looking as a young man; his skin was now sallow and lined in his forty-third year. He had a nervous habit of drumming his fingers and biting his lips. He gave the impression of one who was very unsure of himself.

Jerome Gibbs was fat and pudgy and wore glasses. His clothes did not fit well and he smoked cigars constantly. Thompson hated cigars, so Gibbs was forced to eschew them for the Wednesday meetings, which made him edgy.

Harrison Edwards was Thompson's brother-in-law. He was dark and quick, usually smiling, and was a natty dresser. He made sure the door was bolted when the clerk left. Thompson liked to hold the meetings in secret.

This meeting was especially secret.

Thompson took his place at the head of the table and rapped briefly. "Take your seats, gentlemen, if you will."

When they were seated, looking at him expectantly, he said, "Your report, Harrison."

Edwards nodded and cleared his throat. "I have arranged for five wagons to be driven to the Holliday Bank. The drivers and the bank employees have been told we are moving items to be stored, bank papers and the like. The gold and cash and important papers will be moved by the bank officers themselves in one heavily armed coach."

"Not too obvious," Thompson said.

"No. We have been moving assets over the last several weeks in secret, and the remainder is small, as you know." Edwards consulted a paper. "I expect no incident. All the preparations have gone smoothly . . ."

Gibbs said, "I'm sure you know what you're doing, JM, but I think it's a mistake to close this bank as well."

"So you have said before."

"But the drought is over. There is no panic. Things are going to get much better." Gibbs tapped his pudgy finger on the polished tabletop. "Closing Holliday I can understand, But it makes no sense to—"

Thompson interrupted. "The decision has been made, Jerome. Please try to live with it." He motioned to Edwards. "Go on, Harrison."

"That's about it, JM. All the arrangements have been made and checked. By this time Monday we will have moved everything of value from Holliday to here."

Thompson nodded and pointed to Tredwell. "Homer . . ."

"All the arrangements have been made to receive it. The cash and gold will come in late Sunday night. I will be here to lock it in the vault. The other wagons will come on Monday morning and we'll put those boxes in our storage area."

"Good." Thompson smiled. "And when everything is completed, brought here and locked up, we can all breathe easier."

Thompson instigated a discussion of loans and policy on other short-term paper. Homer Tredwell had been head of the loan department for a year or more and led the talks, making copious notes, then Thompson adjourned the meeting, asking Edwards to stay behind a moment.

When the others had gone and the door was closed, Thompson said, "I want you to go back to Holliday, have the building cleaned and repainted and put it up for sale. We no longer need it."

"Yes. I've already talked to an agent."

"Very good. Then you will discharge all the bank employees, including the officers. Make sure all their pay is up to date. We'll have no further need of them of course."

"Yes, I will. It's too bad . . ."

Thompson drew down his lips. "I cannot pay them if they do no work, now, can I?"

"No, of course not."

"I am not my brother's keeper. Discharge the lot of them. Give them references if they wish it."

Edwards nodded and went out.

The Holliday Bank was closing because it was barely breaking even and in Thompson's eyes, its future was bleak. The recent drought had ruined many farmers and cattlemen, and loans were not being repaid. Also, not enough new money was coming into the territory.

But the Gunnison Bank was another thing. It was prospering. Its future, Edwards thought, along with the other bank officers, was excellent. It was J. M. Thompson who had the jitters and who insisted they must retrench. It was his idea alone to move to Farrington, where he had established his first bank. The older he got the less he wanted to risk anything. The country, he said often, was not growing as he had anticipated.

But in the opinion of all the bank officers, Thompson heard what he wanted to hear. He listened to advice with half an ear, and his whims were legendary.

He was cordially hated by most of his employees for his biased attitudes, and no one expected anything from him but harsh treatment. He was quick to dock their pay for lateness, mistakes or any infringement of his rules, and every employee knew his job was constantly on the line. Thompson seemed to relish firing people.

Harrison Edwards, though he had married Thompson's sister, still knew he held no special position in the bank, though the other officers thought he did.

But Harrison was very efficient. Most of the assets had been removed already from Holliday. Edwards would return there on the morrow and close the bank for good. He would make Thompson's excuses, fire the employees and see that all the other property was removed, packed and loaded on wagons. He would pay off everyone and arrange for the sale of the building.

Holliday was a farming community and people went to bed early. Even the saloons closed early. It would be no chore to load the wagons and move out before midnight, and no one would be the wiser. There was little crime in Holliday at best, all very petty . . . mostly drunkenness. Edwards expected no holdup men.

However, the move from Gunnison all the way to Farrington would be something else. That would be very interesting to a criminal.

To close the bank and move its assets, gold, paper and greenbacks a hundred miles over open prairie would be a huge problem and a vast security headache. For one thing, the local newspaper was sure to make a hurrah over the bank closing; they had already mentioned the Holliday Bank closing with no enthusiasm and a few jibes at Thompson.

That kind of advertising might well draw the eyes of criminals.

So any information about dates of closing was the deepest secret. If any breath got out it could mean big trouble—and loss. Edwards knew that if he lost the bank any money at all, Thompson was certain to fire him.

Thompson had stated that he wanted to be in Farrington in six months. Harrison Edwards was in charge of the move. If everything went smoothly, that was a likely figure. But it was a long, dangerous move across the prairie, and a few hills. Edwards had pored over the route and had driven it four times in a four-horse coach.

There were actually two main roads that could be taken, though one was weedy and seldom used and in part almost nonexistent.

But he would give the Farrington move his full attention

as soon as the Holliday move was completed to JM's satisfaction.

Jerome Gibbs and Homer Tredwell went into Gibbs's office from the meeting. Gibbs slid behind his desk and fished out a box of cigars, offering one. Homer shook his head and Gibbs lighted up.

"He's going to get rid of us, you know. As soon as the move to Farrington is finished."

Homer nodded. "I've been thinking about that. I'm afraid you're right."

"You bet I'm right. JM's got a group of officers now, in Farrington. He doesn't need us . . . same as he didn't need those in Holliday."

Homer sat down listlessly. "And there isn't a damn thing we can do about it."

"Yeah, it's his bank." Gibbs puffed hard on the cigar. "It's stupid, the move. Thompson's an old woman. He gets worse every year."

"You've known him longer than I have . . ."

Gibbs sighed. "He's afraid of his shadow. He's like a mother hen sitting on her eggs. He ought to retire and let us run things."

"And stay in Gunnison."

Gibbs waved the cigar. "Right. And stay right here in Gunnison."

Homer agreed. Privately he had been wondering, since he had been told the move was imminent, how he would survive. He was certain Gibbs was right, that they would be fired. Thompson was a pompous ass who cared nothing for his workers. No one was close to him. And his wife was just as standoffish.

Everyone in town would cheer if some bushwhacker put a slug in his gut.

★

Chapter 2

Harrison Edwards had planned well. He closed the Holliday Bank, had his workers take the remaining specie, gold and other assets to Gunnison without incident, then moved the rest of the papers, records and property.

It all went like clockwork. There was no trouble or confusion and even JM was pleased—a very difficult thing to arrange.

Edwards then paid off the employees, the part he dreaded most of all, and put the bank building up for sale. The local *Ledger Bulletin* made a big story out of the bank closing and to Edwards's annoyance went so far as to speculate whether or not the Gunnison Bank would go the same route.

When Thompson read the paper he raged for an hour or two.

Holliday completed, Edwards then turned to the Gunnison move, on Thompson's orders. He hired a foreman, Matt Kaper, to boss the drivers and guards. And with Kaper he spread out the map to Farrington. Kaper had also traveled the route and he concurred; they would use the southern road.

Kaper asked, "How many wagons do you figure to use for the first train?"

"I think we should send papers and property the first time out. Two or three wagons."

"Sort of a trial run . . .?"

"Yes." Edwards's finger traced the long road. "That damned newspaper story may have alerted the wrong people."

"I was about to ask about guards."

"Yes. I've been thinking about that, too." Edwards patted his pockets for a cheroot. "If we send a lot of guards, the wrong people will wonder what's in the wagons, won't they?"

"They certainly will . . . no matter what. If they know they're hauling bank property."

"So what do we do about it?"

Kaper said, "One of several things. First, we can arm the drivers and the guards, horsemen to ride with the wagons and horsemen out to the sides, just like we did in the army. Plenty of guards."

"What's the second?"

"Camouflage."

Edwards looked at him and lit the cheroot. "Go on."

"We pile sacks of potatoes or corn or anything over the load. Make it look like something else."

"And send guards, too?"

Kaper sighed. "That's the trouble. If we send mounted men with a camouflaged wagon or two, people will wonder why men need to guard sacks of spuds."

"Yes. It defeats the whole thing . . ."

"So I guess the best thing is guards. A half-dozen mounted, well-armed men should do it. Arm the drivers as well and keep the times of departure a secret."

Edwards nodded, considering. He liked the idea of camouflage. If they made the wagons look so poor no one would give them a second glance . . . But he hated to take the chance of sending wagons loaded with gold without guards. If something happened, Thompson would have his hide. And no excuses. Money was precious to JM.

He shook his head. "It's a damn long way to Farrington. I think our only bet is secrecy and guards."

"I think you're right," Kaper said. "Secrecy is the ticket. You should be the only one to know the exact times of departure. You and no one else, not even me. Not even JM."

Edwards smiled thinly. "Make me responsible, huh?"

"Well, you are now."

Edwards nodded. That was true enough. JM had given him the job and expected him to do it.

He went down the hall to report to JM what had been decided.

People halted in their tracks; men and boys stared, eyes popping out, as Jessica Starbuck stepped off the stage in Gunnison. No one had seen anything like the honey-blonde, green-eyed beauty who smiled at each of them, batting long black lashes.

This vision was dressed in blue jeans that were molded to her marvelous backside, and a lacy white blouse that contained pleasantly bobbing breasts as she walked to the hotel, followed by a grinning young lad with her luggage.

No one noticed the tall, dark man who walked behind the boy. He wore a slight smile, as though he had seen all this many times before. Had Jessica not been there he might have drawn stares on his own. He moved with catlike ease, wearing a dark cotton shirt, leather vest and black jeans. He was apparently unarmed and might have been an Indian or a Mexican, but he was neither. He might have been an

Oriental, but he looked nothing like the Chinese laborers people were used to seeing.

He was in fact, half-Japanese. And possibly the most dangerous man in town.

J. M. Thompson had had some connection with Jessica's father, Alex Starbuck, at one time. Of course Alex had known thousands of people, but Jessica, finding herself so close to Gunnison, had come here to say hello, trusting that J M had been a friend. She would find out soon.

She and Ki were on their way home to Texas for a rest, having just exerted themselves mightily in a silver mountain quarrel. Gunnison was such a peaceful little town . . . what could happen here?

They put up at the Gunnison Hotel. The bug-eyed clerk blinked and stuttered, watching Jessica sign her name in the register. He gave her a key with trembling fingers and watched her climb the stairs to the second floor, his mouth hanging open.

Ki had practically to pinch him to bring him back to reality, and then his eyes did not focus properly for a moment.

They were given rooms across from each other on the second floor, and when she was settled, Jessica sent a boy with a note to J. M. Thompson to say she was in town and would be delighted to visit a moment with him.

Thompson's return note said he was very glad to hear from her and would take great pleasure in her company for dinner that evening at the Summer House, a restaurant near their hotel.

Thompson, reading Jessica's note, said to Harrison Edwards, "Have you heard of her, Jessie Starbuck?"

"Yes . . . I believe I read something . . ."

"She doesn't mention her half-Japanese partner, but he is probably with her. I understand she goes nowhere without him."

10

"Half-Japanese? That's odd."

"Yes. He's a master of some oriental fighting system—I don't quite understand it. Apparently it's something to do with hands and feet alone. I saw a demonstration once a long time ago." Thompson frowned at the note. "It might be a good idea to ask for their help."

"What for?"

"To watch the goddam shipment! I want it to go through to Farrington without trouble."

"It will, JM. It will."

Thompson grunted. "You're damned right it will." He put the note in his pocket.

Jessica unfolded a dark blue gown from her suitcase and hung it to brush out wrinkles. She was fussing with her hair when Ki appeared.

"Am I going with you?"

She looked at him in surprise. "You certainly are!"

He sat in an easy chair. "Tell me about this Mr. Thompson."

"I know very little about him. I remember him slightly as a fish face—"

"A fish face?"

She smiled. "Little girl talk. He was an acquaintance of my father's. I haven't seen him in years. But we will have dinner and let him talk, then get back on the train tomorrow. Agreed?"

"Fine."

The Summer House was the finest restaurant in town. It had a shimmering ceiling with ornate lanterns hanging from it, potted plants artfully arranged and tables with crisp white cloths. There was a bar to the left, its decor black and red. Jessica had seen nothing like it west of Kansas City. Someone had taste . . . rare for the outlands.

When she mentioned Thompson's name to the young man

11

who met them at the door, he led them at once to a secluded table, saying he expected Mr. Thompson at any moment.

They were barely seated before Thompson arrived. He was more stout than she recalled, his florid face wreathed in smiles. He kissed Jessie's hand gallantly and shook with Ki, delighted, he said, to meet him and charmed to greet her again.

She said, "I was hoping to meet your wife . . ."

"She is not feeling well, I'm sorry. A touch of cold or something of the sort. The doctor was vague." JM snapped his fingers and asked for the wine list.

They chatted about nothing in particular. JM had heard of their exploits from time to time, he told them. Jessie said they did their best to keep them from being publicized . . .

Jessica was surprised to see that the menu was in French, here in this far Western town. She wondered if Thompson had ordered it specially, just for them. Was he trying to impress them? She noticed the amusement in Ki's dark eyes; he probably thought so, too.

She ordered *L'Estouffat Lamande* . . . which was pot-roasted beef and red wine.

And she bit her lip to keep from smiling at J. M. Thompson's face when Ki, without turning a hair, ordered *Foie de Veau Menagere* and discussed the selection with the waiter, in excellent French.

Thompson then chattered about the bank closing in Holliday, saying that the operation of a bank in the untamed West was fraught with difficulty, that it took the very strong to survive. And he hinted that he had something of importance to discuss with them if they would stay over a day.

They agreed, and when they returned to the hotel, Ki bought a copy of the local weekly and they went up to Jessie's room.

and pointed to a chair. "What do you think?"

Ki shrugged. "I don't see any problems. He wants us to make sure the shipments get through . . . but we can only do so much. We're not in charge."

"That's right."

Ki sat down. "It all depends on what kind of man Harrison Edwards is. If he's the wrong kind, *then* we have problems."

"We'll stay out of his way as much as possible."

Ki nodded. "Then you want to get involved?"

"If we can help . . ."

"Oh, I think we can do that. I see our part of it as scouting, when the shipments go across the prairie."

"I agree. I don't see how Edwards can object to that."

They went to the bank the next morning and met Edwards in Thompson's office. Harrison was a slim man and, as ever, was well-dressed. He bowed to Jessica and shook hands with Ki, and they seated themselves.

JM said, "This is a little meeting to clear the air. Harry is in charge of the move to Farrington. There will be no question of that. Are we all agreed?"

Jessie and Ki nodded as Edwards glanced at them. He smiled.

Thompson continued: "Jessica and Ki will work as scouts. They will make sure no enemy will attack the wagons—if that is at all possible."

Jessie said at once, "That is of course impossible, JM. Two people cannot be everywhere at once. The prairie between here and Farrington is vast. You said yourself it would take a troop of cavalry."

Thompson sighed. "You will do the best you are able. Now, Harrison, what do you want to do next?"

"I would like to go over the route with these two later this afternoon . . ."

"Fine." Thompson looked at Jessie, who smiled and nodded. She rose and Ki followed her to the door.

Edwards said, "I'll come to the hotel later."

"We'll be waiting." They went out.

Edwards said at once, "She's a beauty, JM, but what the hell do we want with her on this job? If a bunch of hard cases show up she'll scream and run to mother!"

"Her reputation says different."

"Do you believe everything they say?"

Thompson moved uneasily. "Do you have any hard evidence that she's not worth a copper?"

"No, of course not. But look at her! How could anyone that beautiful be worth a damn in a fight? She belongs in a bed, naked."

Thompson sighed deeply. "I tend to agree, but I'd like to give the two of them a chance. They *do* have a marvelous reputation. Try to put up with them."

The map that Edwards spread out on the hotel table was not very detailed. It had been put together by several people who had traveled the area, and all of the indicated mileages were guesses.

But it showed two main roads to Farrington. They were noted as the northern and southern routes, and Edwards had selected the southern for the move, though it was the most traveled.

"I've been over both roads and I think the southern is the most direct."

"It's about a hundred miles," Ki said, "with no other towns in between."

"Yes, it's mostly prairie," Edwards traced with a finger, "with hills along here."

Jessica asked, "Is there any chance of getting the army to help?"

18

"JM has tried and they cannot spare any men—they say. The cavalry is spread very thin. It's up to us to defend ourselves."

"What kind of wagons will you use?"

Edwards made a long face. "Any kind so long as they're sturdy. It's a long trip over terrible roads."

Ki said, "I suggest you use several types."

"Yes, that's been suggested. You mean for camouflage."

"Exactly. And put your mounted guards in farmer's clothes."

Edwards rolled up the map. "We've been over this before. It comes down to many guards or very few guards and much camouflage."

Jessie said, "Secrecy is very important. If no one knows when the move will be made . . ." She shrugged. "It would be difficult for a thief to meet the wagons."

"Yes, of course. I fully agree. But all the same, I want the wagons heavily guarded . . . and so does JM. The guards don't have to ride beside the wagons, but they must be close by."

"You are in charge," Ki said, glancing at Jessie. "It will be done as you say."

Homer Tredwell knew his job, did his job at the bank as well as anyone could do it, but he was an ineffectual man. From early life he had gotten by, taking the paths of least resistance. In college he had studied in a desultory fashion, and when examinations came that he knew he would fail, he had purchased his grades—had been able to purchase the answers to questions because he had a very generous father and a loving, doting mother who gave him rather more spending money than most young men received.

He majored in business and banking, and though his grades were fair, his competence was not. Life was too easy. If he wanted something, he had only to ask. But over a period of time he learned enough—he could hardly help learning—and when he left school he worked in several banks, did accounting and loans and drifted west.

When he arrived in Gunnison, J. M. Thompson offered him a job. He needed a loan manager . . .

Homer was married by then. He had married, three years before Gunnison, a woman who reminded him of his mother. Her name was Joanna Gibson. She came from a good family . . . though her father had taken to drink in later years and had lost a high position in an eastern state government.

It occurred to Homer, after an unsettled year of marriage, that his bride had been desperate to marry. Though of course she denied it.

And she proved to be a climber. Nothing he did quite satisfied her, especially in bed. And she had the poor judgment to mention it, so that it drove a solid rift between them.

She also hated living in the territory, when he took her to Gunnison. He did not make enough money; he was in a job that had no future . . .

Most of all, she wanted to return to the East, and she never let him forget it. She was not a nag, but the matter seemed to turn up in conversations quite often, he thought.

Many days he dreaded going home after a long day at the bank, lest she start on that theme again. He took to stopping at the Red Slipper for a quick one.

And that way he met Lucille. She took him up to her cubicle and relaxed him. He was sometimes so relaxed that he could hardly get his clothes back on.

Homer knew he was in a rut, but he did not mind it. It was a rather comfortable rut. If it had not been for J. M. Thompson he might have been reasonably happy. JM was worse than Joanna by far.

It was during one of Joanna's bitchy tirades, wanting to return East, that Homer let slip the secret. She had been expounding on how much she hated Gunnison, and he told her, without thinking, that they were moving to Farrington, a much larger town.

It stopped her in her tracks. "What?"

He sighed. "I'm not supposed to tell you. It's a secret."

"Tell me. You're moving the bank to Farrington?"

He pleaded with her. "Don't say a word of this to anyone!"

"I won't." She stared at him. "So some of the rumors *are* true. The bank is moving."

"Yes . . ."

"*When* is it moving?"

"I don't know. If JM finds out I told you, he'll fire me!"

"Don't worry, I won't tell him."

"Or anyone else."

"Ummmm."

"For God's sake, don't get together with any of those women from the bank and tell them you know."

She shouted at him. "Stop treating me as if I were a child!"

"Then don't worry me to death."

She ignored him. "So the bank *is* moving . . ."

After Homer left for work in the morning, Joanna sat in the kitchen over a cup of coffee. The bank moving to Farrington, a larger town, was the best news she'd heard for a long time.

Homer had told her that the move from Holliday had taken months of planning and doing, and it had been a comparatively easy move. Lugging everything to Farrington would be damned difficult and probably perilous, and it would take a while.

Well, she was for it, whatever.

● ● ●

A few weeks before she had been after Homer to paint the stable. It was so shabby, she was ashamed of it. He would not do it himself, but he gave her permission to hire someone for the job.

She tacked up an ad in the general store, where other ads were placed, and several men came to apply. She picked Virgil. He called himself Virgil Smith. He was a younger man than Homer, and obviously tougher, and obviously unschooled. It was apparent, she thought, that he tended to use force rather than brains.

She hired him to clean out the stable and paint it. And during those days, she had gone outside to watch him work and had felt a certain excitement in his maleness. He was a tiger where Homer was a house cat.

Then one day, when she entered the stable, she found him naked, changing clothes. She gasped, and he stared at her for a fleeting moment, then without a word he grabbed her and pushed her into a pile of straw and was atop her in an instant, pushing her legs apart.

It was rape. He held her mouth closed—for a moment —and then she was gasping and panting and holding onto him with desperation as he pounded into her.

It happened so swiftly—and expertly—that she was being had before she could yell. And then she did not want to yell! He made her like it. She had never experienced anyone like Virgil before, and she discovered something about herself that day. She absolutely hungered for a man who could dominate her.

Virgil dominated her every day after that—in her own bed. He came and went through the alley. Every house in their section had stables on alleys. Horse handlers, drivers and workmen of various kinds constantly used the alleys, walking or driving their rigs. No one noticed Virgil.

22

He was younger than she, reasonably good-looking, dark, and incredible in bed. He had a few scars on his face and more on his body. He told her they were the results of work accidents. He did not tell her he was wanted by the law and was taking odd jobs as a cover. He did not tell her of the years he'd spent in prison for armed robbery and other crimes.

With her he controlled his temper; she thought him marvelously well behaved for a man of his class. He was obviously uneducated. She did not know he had applied for the stable job because he knew her husband was a bank officer. Virgil played percentages; something might come of it.

She gave him money, over and above the agreed price she would pay for painting the stable. She never asked what became of it, because she came to fear that one day he would be gone and she would never see—or feel—him again. She wanted to tie him to her.

And then Homer made his slip about the bank.

It changed things.

Over the several months Joanna had been bedding Virgil she had gradually realized he'd had brushes with the law. Of course he always made it sound as if the law were persecuting him, but she knew he did not fear lawmen—or anything else.

She also mulled over her fate, the fate that had sent her Virgil at this particular time. The Gunnison Bank was preparing for a long move across the open prairie, just at this particular juncture . . .

Virgil, she was sure, was exactly the man for doing something about it. If she played her cards right, she could become rich—and rid herself of her husband, Homer, at the same time. All she had to do was find out from Homer when the gold was to be moved.

Then, if she could talk Virgil into intercepting it . . .

She sat up in bed and told Virgil a story. What if, she said, a great amount of gold and greenbacks was being moved from one place to another in wagons. Could someone manage to obtain these riches without too much trouble?

He said at once, "Of course. That would be easy."

It was the right answer. "But what if there were armed guards?"

He grinned at her. "That's no problem, missy. You hire a couple of men and you find a good ambush spot. The thing about an ambush is—surprise. Surprise is more'n half the battle."

Virgil was delighted with the conversation. It was what he had hoped for. It was apparent to him that she had something definite on her mind.

She said, "But would it be easy to hire several men like that?"

"Hell yeah. If you know where to go t'find 'em."

"And you know?"

He smiled at her. "All right, missy. What kinda game are we playin'?"

"Tell me. Could you hire men who would shoot down other men?"

"You can hire men to do almost anything. You just gotta pay 'em enough."

"And you know where to find them?"

He looked at her, head on one side. "You never ast me them kind of questions before. It sounds like you got something in mind. . . ."

She took a breath. "Did you ever hold anybody up?"

He regarded her soberly. "You mean with a gun?"

"Yes."

"All these questions got something to do with that money bein' moved from one place to another you were telling me about?"

24

She admitted it. "They're going to move the Gunnison Bank to Farrington. That's a hundred miles away."

He stared at her. That was better than he had hoped! "And your husband knows when?"

"I suppose so . . . I haven't asked him anything about it, but he's a bank officer. He ought to know."

Virgil smiled broadly. "You 'n me, we're going into business, missy?"

"Did you ever hold up anyone with a gun?"

"You ain't a Pinkerton, are you?"

"Yes, I am."

"Then let's see your badge." He grabbed at her and they wrestled, falling on the floor. She jumped up and he chased her back onto the bed. Holding her arms tightly, he slid atop her and gazed down. "You goin' to arrest me and throw me into jail?"

She slid her legs about him. "You're under arrest right now."

He laughed. "What'd I do to get arrested? You got to have a charge."

"You just said you'd ambush the bank wagons to make us both rich. Then you'd take me to New York—"

"Did I say all that?"

"That's what you're going to do, isn't it?"

He leaned down and kissed her, feeling her hand reaching for him, to fondle him. "Yeah, that's what I'm gonna do."

Then he slithered atop her again.

Chapter 4

They lolled in bed for several hours. He dozed, then got up to find a cheroot and lay back down to smoke it, cuddling her with one arm.

She said in a dreamy voice, "Did you really hold up anybody with a gun?"

He glanced at her in surprise. "I thought you forgot all about that."

"No. Tell me about it."

He puffed smoke and watched it rise up in the darkened room. "I hadda do it a few times when I was flat broke. There's nothin' to it."

"I'd be scared to death!"

"Naw, you ain't scared. You got the gun, ain't you?"

"The other person could have one, too."

"Well, the thing is, you pull the gun first and hold it on him. He don't have a chance that way. Then you just tell 'im to hand over 'is money and that's all there is to it."

"And you did that several times?"

"You still a Pinkerton?"

She poked a finger into his ribs. "I sure am. Stick 'em up!"

He howled. "You got me . . . Whatchoo gonna do with me?"

"You're going to jail."

"Izzat so? Where's this here jail?"

She giggled. "Right in this bed."

"Well, that's the best jail I ever been in."

She was surprised. "You've been in jail?"

"Well . . . just a little one. Little crackerbox jail once." It was none of her business how many jails he'd been in—or that he'd spent twelve years there.

"Is it bad in jail?"

"Sure, it's bad." He put out the cigar and cuddled her, cupping a bare breast. "Tell me about the bank move. How much money will there be?"

"Well, Homer says since they moved the bank from Holliday, all the assets are here in Gunnison. They'll have to move all of them. It'll amount to hundreds of thousands."

He whistled. "Hundreds of thousands!"

"Yes, in gold and greenbacks."

It awed him. He had never been involved in anything that big! "When are they gonna move it?"

"I don't know."

"Well, find out! That's the most important thing!"

"Homer says it's a secret."

"Sure, it's a secret, but you said your husband is in the know."

"Can't you just watch the bank?"

"Jesus, that won't be easy. You got to sit and watch it for a month maybe. It wouldn't be so bad if I knew within a day or so . . ."

"I don't think Homer knows. JM does of course . . ."

"Who's he?"

"The bank president."

"You s'pose there's as much as a million dollars to be moved?"

She made a face. "I guess so . . ."

"Your husband won't ever know?"

She shrugged. "He might. I don't know. It takes a lot of preparation to move a bank. I guess everyone who works there will know it's coming . . ."

"Yes, but I gotta know within a few hours. I got to know which road they're takin', too." He swung out of bed and began pulling on his pants.

She dressed on the other side of the bed. "I'll keep after Homer . . ."

When they went into the kitchen, she heated the coffeepot and poured two cups. "What do you say, Virgil?"

"About the bank shipment?"

"Of course . . ."

"Well," he smiled, "we in it together, huh, missy? You get the information and I do 'er." He slapped her bottom. "Then we hit the high spots with our million dollars."

Virgil left the house feeling exuberant. A million dollars! Even if she were guessing and it was only half of that, he ached for it. Never before had he been involved in anything that paid him more than a few thousand. And usually he had to split with someone.

He knew where Farrington was, about a hundred miles south—and no towns in between. It was ideal for a fast raid, then get away in almost any direction. If he did it right they'd never have a clue.

He would hire two or three men—probably two would do it—and ambush the wagon train. Then he'd pile the loot into one wagon and disappear. Well away from the scene, he'd pay off the two helpers and head east.

And forget about Joanna, too. With that much money, he could have women by the dozens. He'd have them two at a time as he had once in a Denver whorehouse.

28

Joanna had no idea what he would do for a million dollars.

But until he learned when the wagons were being sent, he had to be cozy with her. Never let her suspect a thing. He would keep her happy in bed . . . and nag her for the date.

But he needed two helpers. Two hard cases not afraid of a little gunplay, who would do what he told them. He had admitted very little to Joanna, but he was a pretty good man with a gun himself. It had been his ticket to prison, in fact. He had shot and killed a man near Pueblo, in a card game, and the law had managed to trap him in a cabin.

Before that he had robbed a stage, in company with a man he'd picked up in a small town as a backup. The man's name had been Charlie Snowden, and they had gone on to half a dozen armed robberies before Charlie had gotten careless. He'd patted a man down for a weapon and overlooked a derringer. The man had shot Charlie to death, and Virgil had shot the killer.

He wished he had Charlie for this job.

There were two deadfalls in Gunnison. They were saloons, but nothing like the Two Barrels in the center of town. These two were dives. One was called the Lucky Spot, the other was Tom's Place. Tom was a big man who had once fought bare-fisted in the ring and never let anyone forget it. Every few days he staged fights in the saloon, men bare to the waist who fought four-minute rounds for whatever purse they could get. Tom passed the hat.

Virgil haunted these two deadfalls looking for his conscripts.

He found one of them quickly, a man named Lyle Geller. He had had a nodding acquaintance with Geller years before, and as they talked, they realized that together they knew a number of men, none of whom Virgil had seen for years.

29

Some were dead and some in jail.

Geller was down on his luck, he said, looking for a score. Did Virge have something good in mind?

Virgil did.

"I need somebody who can keep his mouth shut and who can follow directions. You figger you can do that?"

"Hell yes," Geller said, scenting money. "What I have to do?"

"First thing, we need one more man."

"Is there goin' to be shooting?"

"Yeah. But we'll be shooting first." Virgil bought Geller a beer. "We going to bushwhack somebody."

"How many?"

"I don't know yet. Maybe five or six."

"When we gonna do this?"

"I don't know that either. It depends . . . I'll tell you in plenty of time. Just say nothing to nobody . . . hear?"

"All right. You payin' the freight?"

Virgil gave him some money to seal the deal and left.

He found Ray Beach four days later in the Lucky Spot. They began talking and knew some of the same people, one or two, and Ray admitted he'd spent a few years in Leavenworth Prison for robbing a federal strongbox off a stage.

He was also living on nothing much and looking for a way to line his pockets. Virgil told him nothing about what he had in mind, except that it might entail gunplay from ambush. Ray agreed to wait and be on call, and Virgil gave him a few dollars and took him to meet Lyle Geller.

They got on well, and Ray moved into Geller's rooming house so they would be close. Virgil promised them a hatful of money . . .

• • •

Jessica and Ki decided to ride the route and see what they could see. The south road was the direct road to Farrington, the road all travelers took. The stage had gone that way once, but service had been discontinued when the stagecoach line had stopped serving towns not on the main road east and west. Gunnison was not.

The road was fairly direct over the undulating prairie. It followed the path of least resistance, going around rises and hills instead of over them, but generally straight. It crossed dry washes and a number of deep gullies where it was obvious that men with shovels had labored to ease the grades. There were no bridges at all.

The lack of bridges was in itself probably the reason the stagecoaches had stopped running between Gunnison and Farrington. In winter, when the washes were raging rivers, no coach could make the journey. And of course, neither could anyone else.

Jessica and Ki were especially interested in places where the wagons might be ambushed, and they found several where even one rifleman could hold up a group.

"He might, if he knew when the wagons were coming," Ki said. "Otherwise he could lie out here in the sun and keep the rattlesnakes company."

"There're other travelers," Jessie said. "He'd have to pick the right wagons."

"Exactly."

There were no farms or ranches or even shacks between the two towns—at least not near the road. They saw a few distant deer and a coyote or two, watching them curiously. Edwards had said the road was frequently traveled. That possibly meant as many as five or six pilgrims or drifters a month.

Jessie said, "Well, if the secret is kept, I don't see there being trouble."

31

"That's the key, that's the absolute answer—secrecy, secrecy, secrecy. And I think Edwards is serious about it, don't you?"

"I had a good impression of him."

They rode as far as Farrington, through the low hills north of the town, where the road meandered and twisted, where there were several brushy gulleys, where they both thought an ambusher would be favored.

"And the wagon crews possibly less alert because the end of the journey was so near," Ki said.

Jessie agreed. "And there's no other easy way into the town."

Ki pointed to the distant telegraph poles, which had not followed the road. "If there is a holdup, they'll cut those wires if they're close by. That'll be the first sign of it in the towns."

Jessie looked at him. "You think so?"

"I would."

"It might be better to leave them intact."

Ki shook his head. "If they cut them there'll be no communication between the towns, and it'll add to the confusion."

"Yes, I suppose so . . ."

They went on until the town was in sight, then halted on high ground to look it over. It was definitely larger than Gunnison, far more spread out. It was also on a railroad. The steel rails swept away, shimmering in the distance.

Jessie said, "Let's stay here tonight. I want to sleep in a real bed."

"Yes. And eat in a restaurant."

She smiled.

Chapter 5

The weekly *Democrat* was delivered to the bank and laid on J. M. Thompson's desk. When he had a moment, JM picked it up, read the boxed item and sputtered. It was headlined, *Is the Bank Closing in Gunnison?*

The editor and publisher of the weekly was Jim Hartigan, an old-timer in the town who was afraid of no one. He did his work with a loaded .44 at his elbow on the desk. He had been known to use it when an irate reader came up the steps with a shotgun.

Hartigan published what he pleased and to hell with those who disagreed with him. He had the forum, they did not, and he took advantage of it. Hartigan had never liked J. M. Thompson much, and he was willing to print a rumor, knowing how much it would offend Thompson.

Besides, he was only asking a question. *Was* the bank closing?

Let Thompson refute it if he could. Actually it was a little more than a rumor. Everyone knew the bank had closed in Holliday and the entire shebang brought to Gunnison. Hartigan had talked to several bank employees who told him that papers and records were being boxed at the Gunnison Bank, exactly as if it were moving also. Thompson had told everyone it was merely routine, but no one believed him. No one liked him, so they were glad to believe the worst.

Thompson denied the story printed in the paper. A number of depositors appeared and drew out their money, fearing the bank was about to fail.

JM screamed and pounded his desk, yelling threats against Jim Hartigan, but it did no good. When Hartigan heard, he only laughed.

Thompson tried to find out who had talked to Hartigan, but he could not. Everyone denied it.

The date for the move could not be easily fixed by Edwards. JM and the bank officers were working long hours to get ready; there was much to do.

Homer Tredwell was often exhausted when he got home late in the evening, but there was little he could tell Joanna. He did not know when the move would be made.

She asked, "Will it be soon?"

"I don't know. Why do you keep asking me?"

"I'm interested in what you do."

He was a little suspicious of that. She had never shown any particular interest before.

She said, "When the bank moves, we'll have to move to Farrington, too, won't we?"

"Of course . . ."

"So we'll have to think about selling this house."

"Ummm." He hadn't thought of that. "Put it in the hands of an agent. But wait till the move is made."

"So find out when the move will be."

He sighed. "All right. I'll try."

He was gratified that she did not ask about after the move. He was positive Thompson would fire all of them. He would probably have to fall back on his accounting skills. He'd either start an accounting company in Farrington or go to work for someone . . . unless Joanna nagged him into going east. And she was sure to try to do that.

Virgil slid into the house every day, from the stable, hoping for word. "Why can't you find out?"

"Because they don't tell him! And I can't keep asking him. He's suspicious now."

Virgil was annoyed. The entire plan depended on one fact, which kept eluding him. Was she keeping it from him? But why would she? He could feel the tension building up. Lyle and Ray Beach would want to know why he was delaying. What could he tell them? He was waiting for a man to tell his wife something? They probably wouldn't believe him.

The truth sometimes sounded weak as hell.

He did not know that Joanna was having second thoughts about him. Was Virgil Smith the right man for the job after all? He talked a good story, he had the wounds and scars, but if he were a successful holdup man, why was he painting stables?

Was she putting too much of her future in his grubby hands? She would never get another such chance.

Of course Virgil was marvelous in bed. But so, she was sure, were a great many other men his age. With more education. She could talk about nothing but sex or money with Virgil. He knew nothing else.

She had a vague, uneasy feeling that she had told him too much, and she could not undo it. She was stuck with him. If she tried to get rid of him—what was he likely to do? He would make trouble.

She had seen glimpses of his quick temper—which he quickly controlled in front of her. And he had admitted to a criminal background. Maybe there was more to *that* than he'd said.

35

And he was getting a gang together . . . as he'd said he would. She had the apprehensive feeling that she'd left herself in a terribly vulnerable position. Virgil had nothing to lose. He *had* nothing at all. But she—she had everything to lose! Position, husband, house—everything that was important to her.

If the thing should fail.

But whatever—how could she keep him from making trouble?

Homer had a pistol—somewhere. She had seen it a few times. She searched the bedroom and found it in a box on the top shelf of the closet. The box was covered with dust; Homer had not touched it for a very long time. Maybe he had forgotten he owned it.

She took it out of the box, a Colt revolver, caliber .32, fully loaded. She laid it on the bed, wondering what to do with it now that she had it. Well, she would keep it handy, just in case.

Virgil had changed since she'd told him about the bank move and the huge amount of money involved. Maybe he hadn't noticed it, but he had become more demanding, and less polite. She could tell—he was greedy and eager for the money. Well, of course, she was, too. It meant getting out of this place and away from Homer. But she knew Virgil was in a state; he had never been close to a million dollars before . . .

But when he had the money—then what? He *was* younger than she was. Would she be able to hold him? Would he run after younger women? Men did those things —she could read the newspapers. She had sudden pangs, anxiety attacks. Maybe he would throw her over when the thing was done. He had come into her life so casually, he could go out of it as easily . . .

She went to the mirror and examined herself carefully.

There *were* wrinkles, not easily visible but there. She fussed with her hair, turned this way and that with a hand mirror and stared at her profile. She was a damned good-looking woman!

But it wouldn't hurt to take special pains with her appearance . . .

Virgil never came into the house at the same hour; he said that if he did, someone might notice. So she never knew when to expect him. Luckily, Homer had not once come home during the day, but even so, she and Virgil had a signal. She hung a towel on the rear door when she was alone in the house and the front door was bolted.

His first question when he came in was always the same: "Did he tell you yet?"

"No."

"Jesus! We got to wait all year?"

"I can't tell him to hurry up and find out so we can rob the wagons."

He embraced her with some of his old ardor. "Yeah, that's right, dolly. We can't, can we?" He kissed her. "I been watching the bank. Nothing's happening."

"You're not obvious, are you?"

He frowned at her. "You going to tell me how to do it?"

"No, no, no, I'm just worried about you."

"All right." He kissed her again, then picked her up. "What say we talk in the bedroom, huh?"

Homer noticed nothing. He got home very late, irritable and hungry. "Damn long hours . . ."

She fixed him a meal and he sat down, sighing deeply. She sat opposite him with a cup of coffee.

"Is everything going well?"

He nodded. "We're about finished, thank God. That goddam JM fussing about everything . . . Nobody does anything right, according to him. I'll be glad when it's all moved and over with."

"Yes. I hope it's soon—for your sake, dear."

"I think it'll be some day next week." He turned to the food and began to eat.

Jessica and Ki reported to Thompson that they'd been over the road all the way to Farrington.

"There's nothing unusual about it," Jessica said. "We saw no one, nothing suspicious—no preparations to ambush the wagons."

Ki agreed. "We think the wagons will go through with no trouble."

"Have you set a date for the first shipment?"

Thompson shook his head, fiddling with his silk tie. "I'm not going to set the date. Harrison is in charge. I'll leave it all to him. So no one will know but him. It's safer that way."

"Very good," Jessie said, surprised that Thompson was ready to delegate authority. She showed none of it on her face. Was he doing it so he'd have Harrison to blame if anything went wrong? Probably.

They left the office and went out to the yard, where Edwards was talking to several drivers. He left the men after a bit and came over to them, saying he was about ready to send out the first shipment.

"Not gold," said Ki.

"No. It'll be mostly records and bank paper, no money at all. I'll send one light spring wagon and two riders with the driver." He lighted a cigarette and puffed nervously. "I'll tell the crew about fifteen minutes before they leave, and I'll stay with them until they go, so no one has a chance to talk to anyone on the outside . . . not even to wave good-bye."

"That's good planning," Ki said, nodding. "Will the men have what they need on the trip?"

"Yes. I have everything prepared for them. The equipment and food is already in the wagon."

Jessie smiled. "I certainly hope J. M. Thompson appreciates you."

Edwards sighed deeply. "He doesn't. He's a—" He stopped and took a breath. "I almost said what I really think!"

Jessie laughed. "Please don't swear, Mr. Edwards."

He chuckled with her and dropped the butt of the cigarette to grind it out with his heel—as though it were a neck.

Ki said, "The wagon will go out at night, then?"

"Yes. It'll avoid the main street altogether."

They returned to the hotel with Edwards's promise that he would send for them when the move was ready to go. It meant he trusted them.

They had supper in the hotel dining room and discussed the bank move. It would probably go like clockwork despite Edwards's nervousness. The secret seemed well kept. Ki wondered if Thompson really needed them on the job. It might prove to be a waste of their time in the long run.

He said, "We have turned up no signs of a plot at all. Nothing. There probably isn't one."

Jessie replied, "We promised JM we'd stay for at least the first shipment . . ."

Ki nodded. "We'll do as we said. But then we can discuss it with him. All right?"

"All right. Then we can go on home to Texas and a vacation."

Chapter 6

Virgil met with Lyle Geller and Ray Beach once or twice a week in the Good Time Saloon, a deadfall on the road north out of town. The two were getting restless with no money coming in and nothing to do.

Ray said, "When's your job, Virge? How long we got to sit around on our butts?"

"Be patient. It's coming."

"You keep sayin' that . . ."

Ray was a slim 35-year-old drifter who had been in and out of jails all his life, mostly for petty crimes, until his one sojourn in a federal prison. He had killed a man in Oklahoma Territory over a card debt, and his left arm still had a purplish furrow from a derringer bullet. He had an open-faced, rather innocent appearance to strangers, but he was dangerous and unpredictable.

Lyle said, "We got no money, Virge."

What little Virgil gave them did not go far. He could get very little from Joanna. It was a tight situation. Neither of them would take a job . . .

After Virgil left them, Ray and Lyle put their heads together. They were getting desperate for cash—and they knew only one quick way to get it. Make a six-gun withdrawal.

Lyle had noticed one particular merchant; his name was on the sign out front: Gabe Finley. He owned a harness and blacksmith shop employing several men. It was a good prospect, Ray thought. They could take Finley, get themselves some ready cash, and Virgil would never be the wiser. Lyle said, "What Virge don't know aint going to bite his ass."

Lyle followed one of Finley's workers into a saloon and got into conversation with him. The man was happy to have someone buy the beers and told Lyle that Finley had hired a gang of men to clear several fields of brush. He was bringing in a herd of cattle.

That was interesting news.

And the weekly *Democrat* agreed with the worker in an article that Lyle and Ray read soon after. Finley, the item said, was to pay for the cattle as they arrived. Cattle were selling for anywhere from fourteen to eighteen dollars a head, the paper said, and Finley was bringing in hundreds. A huge amount of money!

Ray frowned over the paper. "It don't say where he's going to pay for them cows."

"It says when they're delivered." Lyle tapped the sheet. "Prob'ly in his office."

Ray nodded. That seemed logical. "You know where his office is?"

"Upstairs over the blacksmith shop."

Ray went to the bar and brought back two more beers. He hunched over the table. "We c'n follow him from the bank to his office, go up behind him and take it away. What you think?"

"Sounds easy . . ."

Ray nodded, sipping the brew. "Shouldn't be nothing complicated about it."

Lyle said, "We don't know when the cows're coming in, though. It don't say in the paper."

41

"We'll have to watch the depot. They'll poke them cows off the cars into the corrals back of the tracks. When they do that, we watch for Finley."

"What about Virgil?"

Ray made a long face. "How long we been waitin' for him t'get off his ass? He talks big, but he ain't done anything yet. This here is solid money in our hands."

"Ummm, we'll have to get the hell out. Can't do Virgil's job . . ."

"That's right. Which you want, a bird in the hand or a turkey in the bush?"

Ray grinned. "I never liked turkey much."

The cattle cars appeared four days later, and Lyle and Ray watched men poke them off the cars with long poles, into the corrals.

Lyle said, "They must be five, six hunnerd. You been countin' 'em?"

"I lost count at about three hunnerd."

"Let's go see where Finley is at."

They knew the merchant by sight, and he did not come down the steps from the office.

The bank closed that afternoon at the regular time, and Finley had not visited it. Lyle said, "When the hell is he payin' for them cows?"

"Can you do it by mail?"

Lyle didn't know. They watched the cattle being driven five or six miles out of town to the fields that the gangs had cleared of brush. But Finley did not appear.

That night Ray said, "Maybe we made a mistake. He prob'ly already paid for them. We got to look in another direction."

"Yeah." Lyle was grumpy and annoyed. The Finley money was already burning a hole in his pocket. "Where the hell we going to look?"

"We got to mosey around and keep our eyes open."

Lyle grunted.

But Finley appeared next morning. He came down the dusty steps from his office clad in a black frock coat, wearing an old brown beaver hat and carrying a brown satchel.

"That's him!" Ray said. He grinned at his partner as they walked behind Finley to the bank and watched him enter. They sat in chairs across the street. It was going according to plan at last.

Except that when Finley came out of the bank he did not return to his office. He disappeared inside the blacksmith shop.

"What the hell's he doing there?" Lyle wanted to know.

In about ten minutes, Finley reappeared from behind the shop, driving a light buggy drawn by a high-stepping bay horse.

"Where's he going?" Ray growled. They hurried for their horses as Finley drove out of town toward the east.

The road turned into the woods, and outside of town, they galloped after the buggy. They caught up with it a mile into the trees. Ray Beach, in the lead, saw Finley's blur of a face as the merchant glanced back, hearing the sounds of fast hoofbeats approaching. When Ray came up even with the buggy he saw that Finley had a revolver in his hand.

But so did Ray. He did not hesitate. He fired twice at point-blank range and saw his bullets kick dust from Finley's vest. They knocked the man off his seat. The body tumbled out and the reins went flying. The bay horse ran off into the trees till the buggy hit a stump and overturned with a crash.

Lyle and Ray jumped down and pulled the body off the path. Both shots had gone into the chest. Finley was very dead.

"He had a gun," Ray said. "Must've dropped it . . ." He kicked the weeds and found it.

Lyle growled, "Le's drag 'im into the trees, get 'im off the goddam trail."

They dragged the body into the brush, righted the buggy and drove it farther into the trees, then unhooked the bay horse and let it wander off. Someone would find Finley soon anyway.

The brown satchel contained a wad of money and some papers. Ray tied it behind his cantle and they rode south and east, unaware that the bank had listed the serial numbers of the bills.

When Virgil went looking for the two, he found they had disappeared without saying a word to anyone. And when he heard that Finley had been murdered and his cattle money stolen, he had a very good idea who had done it.

And now his gang was missing.

The day he learned Lyle and Ray were gone, Joanna told him her husband had said the move would be made sometime next week. Everything at once! Jesus! Now he had to get another gang together in a hurry!

And he found it impossible.

He finally settled on one man, Joel Dewey. Joel was young, maybe nineteen, and he had just come out of a house of correction where he'd been put for stealing a horse. He was skinny, black-haired and had a face like a closed fist. But he was willing if not terribly bright. However, he did not own a gun. And he had no money to buy one.

"I know where I can steal one," he said.

The woman who ran the rooming house where he lived had a pistol. He had seen it when a boarder had cleaned and oiled it for her. She kept it somewhere in her bedroom at the back of the house.

44

"All's I need is a few minutes in there and I'll have it. The trouble is, she keeps the goddam door locked when she goes out."

"What about the windows?"

Joel bit his lip. "I dunno. I'll look at 'em."

That night, when the woman was in the kitchen, cooking supper, Joel slipped around to the back of the house and tried both windows. One was unlocked. He glanced around; the yard had a board fence and no windows overlooked it. He pushed the window up and slithered over the sill.

It took him two minutes to find the pistol. It was under her mattress, at the head of the bed. He shoved it into his belt, climbed back out of the window and closed it silently, grinning.

He hid the revolver under some bushes at the side of the house and went back inside to have supper with the others. That night he passed the gun to Virgil to keep for him.

When the woman discovered the pistol was gone the next day, there was a fearsome ruckus. She shouted through the house, "Who stole my goddam gun?"

She searched every room, especially Joel Dewey's, without finding it. Joel looked innocent, watching her go through the bed and mattress. He spread his hands. "I didn't even know you had a gun."

Harrison Edwards was ready to send out the first wagon. He said nothing to anyone during the day but sent a boy to the hotel with a sealed note to notify Jessica and Ki.

In the middle of the evening he made his rounds as usual and backed up the light spring wagon to the bank's rear door. With Jessie and Ki, he carried out the boxes and loaded the wagon, pulling a tarpaulin over the load, fastening it down.

That done, he left Jessica and Ki with the wagon and

went for the driver and two guards himself. He brought all three back, heavily armed, and all six of them rode out quietly to the Farrington road without seeing anyone.

Two miles down the road Edwards halted them, bade the driver and two guards luck and turned back.

Jessie and Ki went on along the road a mile or more in front of the wagon. The night was quiet and cool and they saw no one at all. They might have been alone on the planet.

When dawn began to streak the eastern sky they halted and waited for the wagon. When it appeared they all halted and got down to build small fires for coffee and breakfast.

The men were armed with rifles and pistols; the driver had a double-barreled Greener, and a pair of binoculars. Ki was impressed that they knew their business. They would be in Farrington in another two days.

After breakfast, Jessie and Ki scouted far ahead and to the sides, looking for trouble or for anyone at all, and found no one. The land was vacant, vast and empty.

Edwards had been exactly right. If no one knew of the move, no one could plan to do anything about it.

They scouted the road through the gulleys and hills and saw no evidence that anyone had been there recently. On the morning of the third day, two horsemen appeared and Jessie and Ki approached them from opposite sides.

"Hold on, gents . . ."

The riders halted and stared at Ki. "Who the hell're you?" Then they whistled, seeing Jessica.

One said, "I think I died and gone to heaven, Jake. Will you lookit that!"

Jessie asked pleasantly, "What's your business here, please?"

The rider wearing a black hat nudged his horse close to

46

her, reached out—and stiffened. There was suddenly a revolver muzzle in his face. "Hey!"

Ki said, "What're you two doing out here?"

The second man started to draw his pistol and stopped when Ki's pistol seemed to jump into his hand and the hammer clicked back.

"We going to Gunnison," black hat said in a surly tone. "What the hell you care?"

"Only that you speak the truth," Ki said.

They held the two on the road till the wagon came along and passed them. Then they bade the two farewell. The two men would probably tell everyone they met about the strange actions of two other people out on the prairie.

The wagon reached Farrington without further incident and rolled to a stop behind the bank, where it was unloaded.

Jessie and Ki went to the telegraph office and sent a wire to Edwards in the agreed-upon code. The shipment had arrived safely.

★

Chapter 7

Four days later a meeting was held in J. M. Thompson's office in Gunnison. JM poured out a dollop of special brandy for each of them, to celebrate.

"Excellent work, Harry. Everything went off without a hitch."

Edwards beamed at the unexpected praise. "Everyone did his job."

They all touched glasses solemnly. Jessie said, "Harrison had it all very well planned."

He smiled at her. "Thanks."

"But now comes the harder part," JM said, looking into his glass. "The specie."

"Yes. I haven't made up my mind how to send it. But I think it might be best to decide at the last moment. Then no one can anticipate me—if I don't know myself."

"Add more guards," JM said darkly.

Edwards shrugged neatly tailored shoulders. "The more mounted guards, the more obvious." He smiled round at them. "I'd like to do it the way they handled the Pony Express back in the 60s. Put a bag of gold and a rider on a fast horse—I'm told they lost none or very few pouches in all the time the ponies ran."

JM growled. "That would take all year!"

"Yes, probably. Too bad. So we're forced to use wagons." Edwards sighed. "But we've proved one thing."

"What?"

"That secrecy is the ticket. We'll keep doing it that way."

Homer Tredwell had lunch with his fellow officer, Harrison Edwards, and commented on the other's obviously good spirits.

"Did you come into an inheritance, Harry?"

"No. I wish I had . . ."

"Well, you're feeling good today."

"Yes, I am." Then Edwards violated his own secrecy rule. He leaned across the table though no ears were close by. "Say nothing to anyone, but our first wagon reached Farrington safe and sound."

Homer's sallow face lighted up. "Well! That *is* good news!"

"Say nothing, Homer."

"Of course not." He grinned. "Maybe old JM will give you a raise."

"Not bloody likely." Edwards sighed. "The son of a bitch expects miracles."

"How many wagons?"

"Just one."

"It went through without a scratch?"

"No trouble at all. Secrecy did it."

"Well, good for you."

When he got home that night, Homer told Joanna, "It's started. We'll be moving to Farrington soon."

"They've started moving the bank?"

"Yes. The first wagon went not long ago."

"Ahhhh, I see. And there are more wagons to go?"

"I suppose so. I heard only that the *first* wagon reached

Farrington. I didn't ask questions. They have everything to be moved under lock and key in a back room."

"Well, that's exciting—"

"Say nothing to anyone!" he cautioned. "This is all very secret."

"Of course not, dear. Are you hungry?"

In the morning, when Virgil came into the house from the stable with his usual question—"Did he tell you?"—she said, "Yes."

"What!?"

"The first wagon went to Farrington the other night."

He yelled, "Goddam!"

"The *first* wagon," she said. "There are others."

"How do you know?"

She shrugged. "Because when they moved from Holliday there were a dozen wagons or more. This move is bigger."

Virgil paced up and down. "Damn, damn, damn. We missed it!" He frowned at her. "Did he say when the next ones go?"

"He didn't know."

"You said he's a bank officer!"

"Yes, but they keep it a secret from everybody."

He swore. "We'll have to watch the goddam bank!" He hurried out without saying good-bye.

That was the moment when she knew—no doubts at all—that the money meant far more to him than she did. He was only using her.

Virgil hurried to find Joel Dewey, and could not. The man was not at the boardinghouse, and no one knew where he'd gone. He was not in any of the nearby saloons. Virgil swore. He was probably in one of the whorehouses—but which one? Jesus, it was early for that . . .

He did not locate Joel till the middle of the afternoon. "Where the hell you been!?"

"Playin' cards. Me and—"

"Jesus! Get your bag together and meet me out on the Farrington road. We got a job to do."

Joel grinned. "It's about time. You bring my gun, hear? How long we be gone?"

"Two, three days. Hurry up."

They met again at the edge of town where there were a number of shacks, mostly deserted. Neighbors were slowly tearing them down for firewood. Virgil and Joel took possession of one and stashed blanket rolls there. Then Joel stayed behind while Virgil rode to the alley behind the bank. He found it deserted. He rode on to a general store and bought airtights, then went back to the shack.

Joel asked, "What we waitin' for?"

"There's a shipment going to Farrington. We'll bushwhack it."

"When's it going?"

"If I knew that we wouldn't have to sit here, for crissakes." What a dumb kid.

"Oh . . . yeah."

Every hour, Virgil mounted and walked his horse along the alley. Nothing.

But long after dark, when he approached the alley, there was an armed guard standing there, motioning him on.

"Can't I go down there?"

"Not tonight, mister."

"It's a public alley, ain't it?"

The guard growled at him. "You lookin' for trouble?"

"Naw . . ." Virgil went on by.

They must be loading the wagons at the bank!

He went back to Joel in a state of excitement. They tied on the blanket rolls and moved out onto the prairie. In an hour or so they could hear the rattles, squeaks and rumbles as the wagons bumped and creaked along the rutted road.

Loaded with money!

They followed the wagons the rest of the night and stopped a mile away when they halted at dawn. The light showed them two wagons, one covered with dirty white canvas. The other was a sturdy farm trap with a tarpaulin stretched over the load.

Virgil could see three mounted guards—so they faced five armed men. Not bad odds if surprise was on his side.

Virgil had long ago picked out the ambush spot. It was a broad dip in the road as it crossed an arroyo. The wagons would have to come down one at a time and be on a flat piece of ground along the sandy bottom for a few minutes.

He and Joel made a wide circle and came back to the road far in advance of the slow-moving wagons. They had plenty of time to take up the best positions at the arroyo. Virgil placed Joel on one side of the road, behind a lump of earth that was probably thirty feet from the path.

He took up a position in the brush on the other side of the road so they would have the wagons and guards in a cross fire.

"Fire at the mounted men first," he told Joel. "You won't have time to reload, so make 'em count."

"All right . . ."

"You fire when I do." Was the kid nervous? Probably. He felt very steady himself. Maybe it was the thought of a million dollars that stiffened his spine.

He spared a few thoughts for Joanna. She would be sitting home waiting for him. Well, she would wait a long time . . .

The wagons did not appear till late in the afternoon, when the shadows were long and he had about decided they had found a good place to stop for the night.

Joel heard them first, his ear to the ground. "They coming . . ."

Virgil nodded. "Fire when I do." He saw the other stretch out full length on the ground, the pistol in both hands, thrust out before him.

Virgil levered the rifle and took his hat off.

There was only one horseman in the lead. He came down the steep slope fifty yards in front of the lead wagon, a rifle across his thighs.

Virgil wanted both wagons in the arroyo before he fired, and he waited . . .

The last, covered wagon was on the slope when Joel fired. The lead horseman was flung back and toppled as the horse bolted.

Virgil swore, sat up and fired rapidly at the other two horsemen behind the covered wagon. He saw one drop out of the saddle, but the other turned, spurred his animal and galloped away.

He fired at the drivers. Both wagons halted and one driver got off a shot, but only one that went into the sky. His wagon rumbled down the arroyo a dozen yards and ran into a boulder that almost turned it over. The other halted in its tracks.

There was a heavy fusillade of shots—then it was still. The smoke cleared slowly and Virgil stood up. The damned mounted guard had gotten clean away. He could see the man disappearing in the distance. Well, nothing to do about that.

Joel was reloading his pistol, looking very pleased with himself.

Virgil snapped, "I told you t'wait till I fired, dammit!"

"Yeah, I guess I got excited, Virge—"

"One of 'em got away."

"He did?" Joel was surprised.

Virgil shook his head, swearing under his breath. He shoved his hat back on and walked down the arroyo, the rifle over his shoulder. The four men were dead all right. Each one had been hit several times.

Each wagon bed was covered with a tarpaulin. Virgil sliced the cords with his knife, pulled the 'paulin off the covered wagon and looked at five wooden crates.

He said to the kid. "See what's in the other wagon."

There was a toolbox under the wagon seat. He found a claw hammer and pried the lid up on one of the boxes. It was packed with greenbacks!

So were the other boxes.

The other wagon held several large crates that proved to contain paper documents. Three small crates held gold. Looking at it, Virgil felt giddy. He had never seen so much wealth in his life. Joel was giggling like a child . . .

They muscled the greenbacks into the smaller wagon, pounded down the lids and stretched the tarpaulin over the load again.

"How much you figger we got?" Joel asked.

"There's too damn much to count!"

"Easy a million dollars, huh?"

Virgil agreed, "Must be a million." He still felt light-headed. He was rich as hell all of a sudden! With shaking fingers he lit a cheroot and puffed, trying to calm his racing pulse. He was rich as hell!

Joel said, "What we do now, Virge?" The kid hadn't thought ahead at all.

The question brought Virgil back to earth. He said, "We got to hide it."

"Hide it?" Joel was astonished. "Hell, I thought we was gonna spend it! Ain't we gonna divvy it up?"

"Not yet, for crissakes. You wanna be caught?" He indicated the bodies. "They'll hang you f'that."

"No I d'wanna get caught." The thought of jail made Joel scowl. "You know a place to hide it?"

54

" 'Course I do. I figgered that out a long time ago. Tie your nag on behind and drive this here wagon up outa this."

Joel did as he was told. They left the bodies and the covered wagon behind. When the escaped guard reached Gunnison they'd send out a posse fast.

Virgil mounted his horse and led the way down the road toward Farrington for another five or six miles, then turned off the road onto the prairie sod, pointing west. After several hundred yards he halted the wagon.

Joel said, "What is it?"

"Stay here." Virgil went back to the road, pulled up some weeds and got down to brush out tracks. He was meticulous about it; a professional tracker wouldn't be fooled, but a posse very well might. He was especially careful about the wagon wheel tracks where it had left the road. That was the critical point.

Satisfied at last, he went back to the wagon. "Let's go."

He led Joel for miles, far into the night, and halted again by a low bluff to make camp.

As they broiled strips of meat before a low fire Joel asked, "Where we going, Virge?"

"There's some old mines a while ahead. I ran onto 'em a few years ago when I got lost on the goddam flats. We'll put the gold in one of 'em and wait till the fuss dies down."

"Wait?" Joel was startled. "Jesus. How long'll that be?"

Virgil shrugged and looked at the other, head cocked. "Say six, eight months."

"Six months!" Joel was dismayed. "Six months! Jesus, Virge, that's forever!"

"Lissen, kid, for what we took today and shootin' them people, they going to look damn hard for us. You know that, for crissakes. I been in prison and I don't aim t'go back. Especially if there's a rope waitin' for me."

55

Joel groaned. "But can't we take some of the money?"

"You bet. We'll take some to tide us over. We got to do that. But not more'n we can explain."

"That's good . . . A couple thousand each?"

"Not that much, dammit. We got to say we worked for wages for it . . . in case we get in a tight spot, you understand. Or maybe we won some at poker. That's got to be our story."

Joel sighed. "All right, Virge. You figger the law's going to find us?"

"Well, I don't see how. But if they do, we can't tell 'em too much." He looked hard at Joel. "Don't tell 'em enough for you to get tangled up in your story."

Joel nodded. "When we come for the money, Virge, we got to have us a wagon or pack mules . . ."

"Lissen, I got it all figgered out. We'll come for the money in six or eight months and we'll bring along a buckboard. We haul the money west to Hilliard, that's a railroad stop."

"That must be a hunnerd mile!"

"More'n that. But I know the town. And I know somebody there, an old man. He's got a barn he don't use no more. We'll build us some new boxes and nail up the gold and label it—something, anything—and ship it east. By then they won't be lookin' for it no more."

"Then we divvy it up when we go east?"

"That's right. You 'n me, we're going to be rich, boy!" Virgil rolled a brown cigarette. "We won't never work again."

Joel grinned. "I like the sound o'that."

Chapter 8

Joanna Tredwell was afraid she'd seen the last of Virgil—now that she could tell him nothing more. She had been very foolish to let herself get into such a mess. Her unhappiness had betrayed her and she regretted everything. Probably Virgil had betrayed her, too.

What if he were caught? Would he implicate her? She sighed deeply and knew in her heart that he would. He would not go down alone.

And Homer . . . what of him? Her husband would never stand up for her when he found out about Virgil. Especially a man like Virgil. He would probably denounce her and move out, and of course everyone in town would despise her. She had made a terrible bed for herself. She had nothing to look forward to but tears and disgust. Her life had suddenly fallen in upon her as though a tornado had whirled down and smashed everything to bits.

And the worst of it was that she had done it all to herself. What in the world was she to do now?

Jessica and Ki circled far ahead of the two wagons, seeing nothing moving on the horizon. The prairie was a vast ocean, empty and lonely. It seemed to stretch on forever with the night sky hanging close overhead, stars just out of reach.

They camped the first night by a small spring that trickled into a green pool where dusty willows grew in profusion. The next morning they returned by a roundabout wandering to the road, and it was plain to see no wagons had passed. They continued along the road to meet them.

They had not met the wagons by nightfall.

"Maybe they halted early," Ki suggested. "I would have thought we'd have seen them by now."

"They're heavily loaded. Maybe a breakdown. . ."

"Yes, that's possible." Ki looked at her and knew she was thinking the same thing, which neither of them wanted to express. That maybe the wagons had been bushwhacked.

He said, "You want to go on tonight?"

Jessie shook her head. "Let's wait for sunup."

They made camp again, off the road, and moved out at dawn. They had gone barely ten miles when they came to the arroyo and the four bodies.

Ki got down slowly. "They were ambushed." He frowned at her. "It means somebody knew. Somebody knew when they were coming."

One guard was missing, as was one wagon.

Jessie said, "Maybe he got away." She looked down the road. "We'd better give a look in case—"

"All right."

She galloped her horse down the road while Ki made a circle on the prairie. A wounded man might have gotten away and they might have let him go . . .

But Jessica and Ki found no one.

It was apparent the killers had taken one wagon to carry the loot. They had opened the boxes containing only documents and left them.

Ki covered the bodies with canvas while Jessie unhooked

the mules and turned them out to graze.

"They had it well planned," Jessie said. "So the secrecy was breached. But where?"

"It had to be someone inside the bank who told them, didn't it?" Ki shrugged. "Who else would know?"

It certainly seemed that way.

If one man had escaped and gone galloping back to Gunnison with the news, someone from the town should arrive soon.

They settled down to wait.

When the telegraph reported that the shipment had not reached Farrington, there was much uneasiness in the bank. J. M. Thompson and Howard Leland, manager at Farrington, were on the wire constantly. The wagons were hours overdue.

Thompson finally called the town marshal and asked that a posse be sent out toward Farrington. Leland asked that one be sent from his end.

The men from Farrington arrived at the ambush point first, led by a deputy sheriff. Jessie and Ki went over the attack with him.

"It was obviously an ambush." Ki pointed. "The bushwhackers fired from here and cut down the bank men before they knew what had hit them—except for one man who got away."

"They never had a chance."

The deputy asked, "How do you know one man got away?"

"Three riders were sent out with the wagons. There're only two saddle horses here. And there were five men altogether."

The deputy sighed. "And all the bank treasure is missing?"

"Yes."

"J. M. Thompson is going to scream about that."

Jessie said, "We're going to see if we can track the wagon. Then we'll go back to Gunnison."

The deputy nodded. "Good luck. But them tracks is prob'ly trampled out by now."

The deputy was right. The road to Farrington was rather well trampled by the posse. They went the other way, toward Gunnison, but in five or six miles could see no evidence that a heavily laden wagon had left the road.

Returning, they went toward Farrington with the same result. By nightfall they had found no place where wheel marks had turned off. Perhaps the wagon had gone on into Farrington. Perhaps it was now in Gunnison.

One thing seemed sure. It had disappeared into thin air. With a million dollars.

With Joel driving the wagon and Virgil roaming ahead on horseback, they continued west, following no path. Virgil guided himself by dead reckoning. When they halted to make a tiny fire for coffee and to eat from the airtights, Virgil repeated: his plan was foolproof.

He shook an iron spoon at Joel. "If we's careful and follow it, we'll never be caught."

"Jesus . . . hiding the money for six months." The kid shook his head dolefully.

"It's got to be done. They catch us with this money, we'll hang, sure as God made little deputy sheriffs. We'll hide the money, then circle around and find some town to hang out in for a while. We'll be drifters. If the law searches us, we got nothing." He smiled at the other. "Without no evidence, they can't charge us." Virgil pointed his finger. "If we keep our mouths shut there's nothing they can do. Hear?"

"Jeez, Virge, I ain't going to say nothing!"

"I'm glad t'hear it. No matter what, the less you say to the law the better off you are. You take that for a goddam motto."

Joel sighed. "But six months is a damn long time . . ."

"Think of it as a damn long safe time. And give a thought to that noose that's a-waitin' for you."

"Don't make fun of that . . ."

"Lissen, in six months the lawmen on the job could be dead or retired or busy as hell on something else. Our wanted sheets will be buried under a pile of other sheets. Then we'll hustle our asses back here, dig out the gold and put 'er in different boxes in Hilliard. Then we'll hit the high spots. Once we git it out'n this country they'll never catch us." Virgil fished for the makings. "Gettin' it out is the hard part."

"We'll do it."

"Sure we will. If we're smart."

Two days later they saw the hills in the hazy distance, and by late that afternoon they were close. They halted in the lee of a low bluff and Virgil came in to the wagon.

"You stay here. I'm gonna have a look around. I found these mine holes when I was lost one time. I figger they got to be close by."

He rode off and was gone until dark. When he came in he had not found them. "They can't be far . . ."

In the morning he led the wagon south into a jumble of red hills. Joel waited there for several hours while Virgil made a reconnaissance and returned. "They're thisaway . . ."

He led back the way they had come, then turned west into a narrow valley that opened out to a flat area with steep sides all about, and Joel saw the mine holes. They were obviously old and were grown over with weeds. On the flat were several shacks tumbling down, filled with weeds and debris, not worth anything but burning.

There was nothing else.

"They was a copper strike here," Virgil said. "But it didn't pay. Cost more to haul it out than mine it, so folks just moved out. I doubt if anyone knows it's here, this place."

They unhooked the mule and made camp in the middle of the flat. Joel chopped at one of the shacks with a hatchet, getting firewood while Virgil toured the area looking for sign. He shook his head when he returned.

"Nobody been here in years. This here place might as well be on the moon." He grinned at Joel. "Just right for us, podner. Nobody'll come near it."

They ate meat and beans and boiled coffee. Virgil pointed with a spoon. "That last mine hole there is the one. We'll put the boxes inside and cave in the entrance so's it looks natural. There ain't no fool going to dig into an old mine like that for the hell of it. Our money is goin' to be safe forever."

That evening they opened one of the boxes and counted out two thousand dollars, and each pocketed half. Joel wanted more but Virgil was adamant.

"No drifter like we're going to be would have that much money 'less he robbed it. Keep thinkin' about that noose."

Joel sighed, wanting to argue more, but Virgil had a steely look in his eye. Joel gave it up. Virgil was right, of course . . .

They hooked up the mule again and drove the wagon as close as possible to the last mine hole, and with much heaving, grunting and struggling, they carried the heavy boxes into the mine tunnel. They put them down a dozen feet from the entrance, then worked for an hour or more caving in the entrance, making it look as natural as possible.

Virgil even transplanted weeds till he was satisfied they had done all they could.

He patted his pockets. "This money got to last us till we come back for the rest. If we spend it we got to get us jobs till the time is passed."

The sight of all the money, packed thickly into the boxes, made Joel's eyes sparkle. He had never seen so much real money before—and half of it was his. When Virgil had opened the box to take out the two thousand, it had begun to sink in what they had. He was honest to God rich! He was going to be able to live a life of ease, to have any goddam thing he wanted and not ask the price.

Virgil sighed, seeing how Joel was excited with the money in his jeans. The kid would probably spend it all in a couple of weeks. Would he be able to keep him in line? Joel had the brains of a shoat. He might be wise to shoot the kid here and now and put him in another of the mine holes. Virgil felt his neck, thinking about it. Would he regret it later?

He growled, "Take that goddam wagon out and burn it. Take it four, five miles from here."

"Hell, why not just leave it here?"

"Because it's evidence. We got to burn it. Don't you figger them bank people will know their own wagon?"

"Oh, yeah, guess they would . . ."

Virgil followed Joel and the wagon for several miles, making sure. Joel stopped in a dry wash, unhooked the mule and turned it free, then hacked at the wheel spokes till the wagon settled down on the sand. He pulled brush and shoved it under the wagon bed and set it afire.

The wagon was tinder dry, and when the fire took hold, it blazed up gleefully. Joel did a good job, shoving the wheels into the heart of the fire, burning everything down to a black, smoldering pile, leaving nothing but fire-ravaged iron fittings that no one could identify.

63

He sifted through the ashes to see that nothing was left, then kicked sand over the lot.

Let some sheriff make something of that.

Virgil smiled his approval. The kid had *some* brains after all. Enough to burn a wagon.

Chapter 9

Jessica and Ki went on into Farrington. They had no real hope of finding the wagon there; it was a large town, after all. There were a hundred places to hide or conceal it. And the raiders had the advantage of being faceless. He or they—however many there were—could board the train when it arrived, right under their noses.

That was a frustrating feeling.

They went to the bank and talked a bit with the manager, Howard Leland. Gunnison had wired him that morning with information. The guard who had managed to get away from the ambush had a superficial wound, a bullet in his hip. He had seen two men firing at him and the others. Only two. He was positive. He had been hit and had ducked behind a wagon and had seen instantly that to return fire was hopeless.

He had not recognized either sniper, had seen them only for an instant, but he could not be shaken on one point. There were two men and only two. Those two had opened up on them at close range; they'd had no chance at all. His escape had been a miracle.

Leland had also received a list of the missing gold and greenbacks. The loss amounted to nearly a million dollars.

Jessie asked, "Could all the money and gold be carried in a suitcase or large carpetbag?"

"No. It would take several large bags, I'm afraid. And the gold would take special handling. It is very heavy and not at all easy to transport unless in sturdy boxes. If you put it in carpetbags you'd break off the handles lifting it."

"So it will be someone shipping heavy boxes—if it is put on the train."

Ki said, "Shipped as freight . . ."

"Yes." Leland nodded quickly. "The sheriff has already been informed of the facts, and I'm told he will wire all depot towns in the area."

"Very good."

Leland looked at them curiously. "Is it possible the murderers would have the nerve to come here into town to board the train?"

Jessie said simply, "We have no idea what they look like. And if there are two of them, they will certainly travel separately."

"You paint a dismal picture . . ."

Jessie nodded. "At this moment all the cards are in the hands of the killers."

They took rooms at the hotel, deciding to return to Gunnison the next morning. If the plot against the bank had inside help, Ki thought, then the bank was the place to look. There had to be an informer.

Jessie agreed. How could it be otherwise? "No outsider had a chance to learn bank secrets."

"We have to find out exactly who knew of the shipments, and that may not be easy. The guilty party will deny all knowledge. We may wind up trying to read people's minds."

"And one thing to keep in mind," Jessie warned, "the people who did this are killers."

Ki smiled. "We've dealt with killers before."

Before they left town they took one last look around, riding through the town, in and out, hoping to catch a glimpse of the elusive wagon. It had yellow wheels and black trim, much scarred. They kept an eye out for newly painted wagons, too, but saw none.

"If it's here," Ki said, "It's inside a barn or stable and someone is repainting it this minute."

They asked questions of livery stablemen and passersby, but all shook their heads. No one had seen such a rig. It had truly vanished into thin air—with the money and gold.

The local sheriff informed them that he was keeping a sharp eye out for anyone who suddenly began to spend money freely, but he stated his opinion that the murderers had planned well so far and probably would not easily turn stupid.

He also told them that J. M. Thompson had offered a one thousand dollar reward for information leading to the arrest and conviction . . . and return of the money.

Ki said, with a touch of tartness, "That's very generous. One thousand to recover a million!"

"He's only a banker," the sheriff replied. "They don't think or feel like ordinary folks."

"JM is not ordinary folks," Jessie observed.

Toward midday they took the road to Gunnison, both slightly nettled that someone had put one over on them. And quite possibly that someone hadn't even known they were on the case. That made it even more annoying.

Virgil and Joel Dewey left the mine holes behind and rode south and west, avoiding towns for days, especially any town on the telegraph. Virgil was certain no lawman could be on their trail. "We covered it too good."

But probably in a day or so even towns not on the telegraph would get news of the robbery and shootings. It would be red-hot news—a million dollars was missing!

So it would be foolish for two drifters to lay down too many greenbacks in a small-town bar. Everyone and his cousin Jake would be scrabbling for the reward and likely to pick on strangers.

"In a big town nobody bothers," Virgil said. "They all got their own troubles. We got to lay up in a bigger town . . . and change our names."

One other thing was on Virgil's mind; he thought about it as they traveled the rolling prairie. It would be very wise of him to stick close to Joel. The other had not proved to be smarter than a can of tomatoes. There was no telling what dumb thing he would do next. Joel did not seem to think farther ahead than his nose.

Virgil was wondering if Joel could keep his big mouth shut for six months. It was a crucial thing. Joel's mouth could put both of them in prison while they waited for the hangman to stretch his ropes.

Several times during the ride, Virgil fingered his revolver as he looked at Joel's back. He could solve the entire problem with one shot.

Once he even pulled the pistol from its holster and slipped his thumb over the hammer. Joel happened to turn his head at that moment, and Virgil clicked the hammer back and examined the rounds in the cylinder as if it were a very ordinary action. Then he peered around at the horizon as if expecting to see a posse.

He shoved the gun back into the leather wondering if he would have gone through with it. Would he regret one day that he hadn't?

At dusk, when they halted for the night to make camp, Joel asked about the future. "What we going to do for six months, Virge?"

"Hell, we going to roll in the hay with some perty

wimmin, drink a lot of rotgut, play some cards and most of all we going to keep our mouths shut . . . that's what. And the time will pass if we don't worry it every goddam minute."

Joel was silent, digesting that. After a bit he said, "What if we runs out of money?"

"I already told you. Then we get jobs to tide us over. We got to act like what we is."

"But it'd be so easy to come back and get more . . ."

Virgil looked at him, almost ready to pull his pistol again. The stupid son of a bitch would do it, too, run back to the mine till he had a goddam trail dug in the sod so anybody could follow.

He said, slowly and distinctly, "We are not goin' back to the mine for at least six damn months. You get that through your head, Joel." He pointed his finger. "I mean it."

Joel sighed deeply and nodded. "All right. If you say so, Virge."

"I say so, and I mean it. I am not going back to prison."

"Me either. I don't want to any more'n you do."

"All right, good," Virgil said. "Then don't be gabbin' about it no more. Keep it off your mind so you won't spill it to strangers."

"Don't worry. I ain't never goin' to do that."

"Hmmm." You better not, Virgil thought. The worry nagged at him.

They came to Alister two days later, a dusty town on the winding Hawly River, a shallow stream full of rocks and weeds. There was no bridge, but the river could be forded almost anywhere, except when it rained. In some respects, Virgil thought, it was like the Platte farther north, a mile wide and an inch deep.

Along the riverbank was a scattering of tents and shacks and cabins that would be washed away in the first flood. The town was farther back, on higher ground. It was a crossroads, a stage station and only fifty miles from a railroad.

Joel wanted to put up at a hotel in the center of town, but Virgil said no, their money would go a lot farther if they stayed in rooming houses, and they'd be a lot less visible.

"Jesus, Virge, you worryin' about money when we got—"

"Stop that talk!" Virgil's face reddened. "We ain't got a goddam nickel except what's in our kicks right now. Dammit, Joe, I told you!"

"Yeah, I forgot . . ."

Virgil growled, sighing. He should have shot the dumb son of a bitch when he had the chance.

A skinny woman named Mrs. Larch rented them a room with two cots. "Two-bits a day and meals extra. How long y'all stayin'?"

"Six months," Joel said.

Virgil glared at him. "We don't rightly know, ma'am. We been driftin' north and would like to set a while and sort of rest up."

In the room he yelled at Joel, "For crissakes let me do the goddam talkin'!"

"Hell, six months didn't mean nothing to her, Virge."

"I don't care. You say as little as possible, hear?"

Joel was hurt. "You sound like you think I ain't got any brains, Virge. I know not to talk about the money in front of—"

Virgil shoved a finger in the other's chest. "Don't even talk about it to me! Dammit, forget we got it! Can't you think for a second before you open your face? Don't you understand? You and me, we got secrets. Damn important secrets and we don't want nobody else to find out about 'em. Nobody!"

Joel's eyes opened wide. "That's right, Virge. We got secrets! We know things nobody else does."

Virgil was surprised. The idea of secrets seemed to make a difference to the kid. Virgil built on it, lowering his voice. "A secret ain't a secret anymore if somebody wrong knows it. Understand?"

Joel nodded eagerly. "Yeah, that's right. Don't you worry, Virge. I won't tell nobody our secret!"

★

Chapter 10

Jessica and Ki returned to Gunnison without incident. On talking with the town marshal they were told he'd instigated a wide search within the town, looking for the missing wagon, but had not turned it up. There seemed to be no clues at all as to the the murderers' identity or whereabouts. They were shadows who had come and gone . . .

The marshal's name was Jack Coleman, and he was the local law in Gunnison. His was a position appointed by the Sunset Merchant's Association. They paid his salary and that of his deputy, and he was responsible to them.

Coleman was an old-timer, lean and gray, with the manner of a man who knew his way around and was afraid of little or nothing. He'd had a world of experience in law matters and was a good politician.

He had not been called in by J. M. Thompson when the wagons had been ambushed, because the crimes had taken place far out of town. His jurisdiction stopped at the end of Main Street. But he knew a bit about the crimes.

When Jessica and Ki were seated in his office, after telling him that they were working for Thompson concerning the bank tragedy, Coleman said at once, "Someone inside the bank was in on it."

Ki smiled. "We think that's a reasonable idea, Marshal. Someone inside the bank had to be in on it. There's no other sensible answer."

Jessie asked, "Do you know the people who work there?"

"I've met all of 'em at one time or another." He got out a cheroot and regarded it. "There's only one of 'em I'd rule out."

"You mean Thompson?"

"No, I mean Jerry Gibbs." He scratched a match. "I can't see him a-rammin' around out on the grass shootin' people. It don't wash." He lit the cigar.

Jessie was astonished. "You mean Thompson is on your suspects list? He's the one who lost all the money in the raid."

Coleman's craggy face wrinkled into a grin. "How you know he did? Because he said so?"

"Well, yes . . ."

"Lissen, I'm not accusin' anybody. I'm just talking. We're talking, us. Huh? Now if I was just gabbing I'd tell you I seen bank presidents run off with bank funds afore. And I figger you read about 'em, too, in the papers."

"Yes, that's true," Ki said. "Nevertheless, Thompson doesn't seem a likely suspect. We know where he was when the murders took place. He'd have had to hire someone to do the job for him. And I'm not sure I believe that J. M. Thompson would trust someone else with a million dollars of his money."

"That's a good argument," Coleman agreed, puffing. "Y'all looked for that wagon, too, huh?"

"We did. But there could be dozens of wagons out there and nobody would find them for years."

The marshal grunted and dropped ashes on the floor. "Of course that wagon don't look now like it did. No more yellow wheels—if it still is a wagon. If I'd done that job,

73

the wagon would be a pile of ashes by now."

Jessie asked, "Then how would they move the gold and specie?"

"Oh, half a dozen ways. I'd've had a couple of mules waitin' out there with a cart or packtrees. I'd transfer the gold onto the mules and head for places unknown after burning the wagon. Now what you looking for?"

"Or bury it," Ki said.

"That's right. Bury it deep and go back for it later when folks has forgot about it."

Jessie asked, "You think that's what happened?"

"Well, I'll tell you one thing. Hauling that gold out of the country will be a problem right now. Anywhere you take it, some lawman is going to want to see inside your box." He pointed to his desk. "I got wires about that already."

They thanked Coleman and went out to walk to the bank. Ki said, "The marshal is right. Hauling that gold anywhere right now is impossible."

"You think it's buried?"

"It's got to be—part of it anyway."

She nodded. "It seems the only answer."

They requested a short meeting with J. M. Thompson when they arrived at the bank. JM was grumpy, his secretary said in an aside to Jessie. And he was right. Thompson looked tired and drawn, as if he had not been sleeping. He demanded to know what they had learned and was obviously disgusted that they knew little.

Jessie asked permission to interview his bank officers.

He said, "I've already talked to them."

"May I talk to them, please?"

He growled, "Go ahead . . ."

Ki asked, "Who besides yourself knew of that particular shipment?"

"That particular one? Only Harrison Edwards. The others

knew about it, but not when it was sent."

"What others?"

"Homer, Jerry Gibbs and Matt Kaper."

"What about the drivers and guards?"

"They weren't told anything. They never knew what was in the boxes. Matter of fact, all the boxes were labeled the same: records. Harrison told them we were only moving bank records to be stored at Farrington."

"Of course now they know different."

He shrugged and grunted.

Jessie thanked him and they left the office. They stopped first at Jerome Gibbs's office, asking him for a moment. The pudgy man had a cigar smoking in a silver tray. As they sat down he said, "I didn't rob those wagons." He took off his glasses and rubbed his eyes. "What can I tell you?"

Jessie smiled winningly. "We didn't think you did rob anyone, Mr. Gibbs."

Ki asked, "How would an outsider know when that particular shipment left here?"

"You mean the exact hour?"

"Yes."

Gibbs shook his head. "No one could. Only Harrison knew. He set the schedule for every shipment, and they were all varied." He put the glasses back on and blinked at them. "Harry's security was very tight. Not even JM knew."

Ki asked, "Could someone inside the bank send information out easily?"

Gibbs puffed on the cigar and made a face. "I don't know. I never thought of trying it. But I tell you once more. The only man who knew what was in that shipment and when it would be sent out was Harrison Edwards. And I tell you further that Harry Edwards is as honest a man as you will ever find in this world. He did not rob that shipment."

Jessie smiled. "We have your word on it?"

He grinned at her. "Absolutely."

Ki said, "Are you married, sir?"

"For nearly thirty years." He looked at the cigar end. "Maybe you suspect my wife? She's about my size. Can you imagine either of us running about on the prairie?"

Jessie smiled and rose. "Thank you . . ."

They talked next to Harrison Edwards. He looked tired; there were deep lines in his face and circles under his eyes. He greeted them with no enthusiasm. "I suppose you want information . . . ?"

Ki said, "We're fishing, hoping something will come to the surface. This is a strange case in some respects, as you know."

"Strange?"

Jessie said, "It's a case where we have no ideas at all about the perpetrators. The man who escaped—"

"Walt Sims."

"Yes. Have you questioned him?"

Edwards picked a paper off his desk. "Here's what he said." He passed the paper over and they read it together. Sims reported that he and the others were fired on unexpectedly. He had had a glimpse of the two men doing the shooting, but he doubted he could recognize either again. He had been hit and had turned his horse behind one of the wagons and managed by a miracle to duck away, out of range. They had not followed him.

Edwards said, "It's not much, is it?"

Jessie asked, "Is he all right?"

"Oh yes. He'll recover nicely. It was not a serious wound. He came straight here . . ."

Ki said, "What about Matt Kaper?"

Edwards drummed his fingers on the desk. "Why don't

you talk to him? I think he's trustworthy. He would have gone along on that shipment, but he came down with a bad cold. Probably the luckiest cold he ever had."

"Where can we find him?"

"Home in bed, I expect."

Jessie asked, "Is it possible that one of your men informed someone on the outside the night the shipment went out?"

"I doubt it. I took elaborate precautions against that very thing. They were all under my eye till they left here. They did not meet anyone along the road—until of course—"

Ki asked, "So what's your opinion?"

Edwards said quickly, "I think they watched the bank and followed the wagons at a distance. There's really no other answer."

"You mean someone watched the bank every night for a month or more?"

"They must have."

Harrison Edwards was married. He swore he'd told his wife nothing at all of the shipments. He was perfectly willing for Jessica to interview her.

When they left Edwards they went to the home of Matt Kaper and talked to his wife. Kaper was in bed, as Edwards had said. They could hear him hacking with the cold and did not bother him. They told Mrs. Kaper they would possibly see Matt later.

The last bank officer to interview was Homer Tredwell. They sat in his office while a clerk went to find him. The sallow-faced man stooped slightly as he walked. He wore an expression that said he was overworked and unappreciated; they had seen such before.

However, he greeted them politely and went round behind his desk to sit with hands clasped before him, waiting.

Ki said, "We're asking a lot of questions, Mr. Tredwell,

of all the bank officers. The first one is, did you engineer the holdup?"

Tredwell smiled wearily. "No, I'm afraid not. Are all your questions as incisive?"

"Perhaps not."

Jessie asked, "What do you know about it, sir?"

"Probably not as much as you two. Harry Edwards planned it all himself—as JM directed. I doubt if any one of us knows what went wrong."

Ki said, "What went wrong is that two outsiders obviously knew exactly when the shipment left here—and what it contained."

Tredwell nodded. "Yes, Harry and I discussed it. He thinks somebody watched the bank." He shrugged slightly. "I'm sure he's right. It sounds like sense to me. No one got it out of Harry."

Ki asked, "You didn't know when it was scheduled to go?"

"No, I did not." He shifted uneasily. "I must add that I did not want to know."

Jessie asked, "Are you married, Mr. Tredwell?"

"Yes, but my wife isn't much of a gunman. I doubt if she knows one end of a pistol from the other."

"And you said nothing to her about the shipment?"

Tredwell shrugged again. "I knew nothing to tell her, as I just said. Harry—Mr. Edwards was the only one who knew."

"Did you discuss the shipment with your wife?"

"No. We discussed the bank moving to Farrington—I suppose everyone in the bank did that. None of us knew what would happen then—I mean in the matter of jobs."

Ki asked, "Did she ask you about the shipment at any time?"

"No. She never did."

"And you wouldn't have told her if she had . . ."

"That's right. JM pounded that into us over and over again."

"I'm sure he did." Jessie rose. "Thank you, Mr. Tredwell."

Outside, on the street, Ki said, "It has to be one of them, doesn't it? One of them informed the killers."

"Yes, and we're getting nowhere. None of them knew except Edwards. Is there something here that doesn't meet the eye?"

Ki gazed along the street. "Possibly. But we've got one more card to play. I suppose we'd best get about it."

"You mean surveillance?"

"Yes. Who's first?"

"I vote for Harrison Edwards."

Edwards lived in a modest two-story house on a tree-lined street only two blocks from the bank. The neighborhood was well settled but not run-down. The house had belonged to his father and had been built by his grandfather. It was the kind of house that remained in a family for generations.

Ki watched for Edwards and saw him leave the bank the next evening. Instead of going directly home, the man turned into the Palace Bar and Grill to stand at the bar.

Ki took a chair on the far side of the half-filled room. Edwards chatted with several men and the bartender while sipping a drink. They all seemed to be old friends. When he had finished the drink, Edwards left.

From the saloon he went directly home without meeting anyone. Ki watched the house for three hours. No one came out. When all the lights were extinguished, Ki sighed and left.

The next evening was the same. Edwards stopped in the saloon for a single drink and chatted as before. There were a few painted girls in the saloon, but none went near him and he evinced no interest in them. When he had finished his drink he left, went home and stayed there.

When Ki reported to Jessie she said, "He doesn't act like a man who just came into a million dollars. It sounds as if Jerome Gibbs was right."

"It could be part of the act. Maybe he suspects he's being followed and checked on."

She pulled down her lips. "Maybe. So you think the killers hid the money and are going on as if nothing happened?"

"That's a very good possibility."

"The robbery-murders took place a long way from here. Did the two killers bring the money and gold here to hide it, or does Edwards—if he's in on it—have an enormous amount of faith in them that they will not double-cross him?"

Ki smiled. "Since you put it that way . . . you're eroding my belief that one of the bank officers was implicated. Except that it has to be one of them."

"It has to be," she pointed out, "because of what we know now. But I have a hunch we only know part of it."

"Hmmmm. I'm afraid you're right."

Edwards's routine did not vary the next day. He did not leave the bank at exactly the same time, but he had his one drink and went home.

Ki leaned on the bar at the Palace Bar and Grill and talked with the barman Edwards had gabbed with. He learned that Edwards had been dropping in there for years, always the same—one drink and out. He never talked with the girls or went upstairs with them. He never gambled and he never talked about bank affairs.

Jessie said to Ki, "Jerome Gibbs told us Edwards is an honest man."

"Well," he replied, "let's see if Gibbs is."

80

But Gibbs went straight home from the bank each day and never left the house again, except on Sunday, when he went to church. And no one came to the house to see him.

"He's honest, too," Ki said.

They gave up on Gibbs and looked into Homer Tredwell's life. And found a different story.

Tredwell led Ki across town to a saloon, the Red Slipper. The first night Ki shadowed him Tredwell did not go into the bar but went directly upstairs to the brothel and stayed two hours.

He was obviously well known there. Ki waited in the bar, chatting with a barman. Edwards always saw one particular girl, the barman said—Lucille. He pointed her out when she came back downstairs, a flashy blonde, the most expensive girl in the house.

Ki managed to get her alone and bought her drinks. He was looking for a friend, he told her, and described Tredwell. "His name is Wilton . . ."

"Naw, his name is Wilson. He's one o' my regulars."

Ki gave her his best smile. "He always liked the prettiest girls."

She accepted the compliment as her due. "You wanna go upstairs, honey?"

"How long have you known Wilson?"

"Oh, a couple years anyway. He's the only one brings me presents."

"Presents!" He was surprised. "Expensive ones?"

She touched her throat. "He give me this necklace . . ."

Ki leaned close and inspected it. It certainly looked expensive.

She said, "I never had it with a Chinaman before. Whyn't you come upstairs? I'll treat you good."

"I'm sure you would. But I have to beg off this time."

She shrugged philosophically. "Next time then . . ." She got up and wandered off.

On the street Ki told Jessie, "He's a regular in there. Gives one of the girls presents."

"I wonder if he has other tastes that require money."

But he did not gamble in the saloon. When he finished with Lucille he went directly home.

His house was in a better neighborhood. The stable behind the house had been newly painted. There were trees and shrubs and it was easy to watch.

The first day they watched the house they saw a man come from the alley, into the stable and into the house. He was young and dark, wearing workman's clothes. Was he a relative or someone doing work for them?

If he did work, it was inside the house. But they heard no hammering. Perhaps he was painting—except that he had arrived with no tools or materials. Maybe they were already inside.

He left the house several hours later. They followed him to a rooming house and learned his name was Virgil Smith. He was a day laborer and did odd jobs here and there, his landlady said.

Virgil went into the Tredwell house again the next day. He stayed several hours and, when he left, walked down the alley three blocks to a row of stores and went into the nearest saloon.

Ki followed him in and managed a close look at the man. Virgil had scars on his face, and looked rough and tough. Did he have a job at the Tredwell house, or was he just going house to house asking for work? It didn't seem to be the latter.

But if he had a job there, what kind of labor was it that allowed him to work only a few hours a day?

Ki watched the house again the next day. Virgil appeared

and went into the house, and this time as he was about to leave, Ki saw him and Mrs. Tredwell embracing and kissing by the rear door.

"He's not a workman," Ki said to Jessie later. "He's her lover!"

"That's very interesting," Jessie observed. "But how does it help us?"

"Well . . . Tredwell has a prostitute at the Red Slipper he buys presents for, and his stay-at-home wife has a lover who comes in during the day while her husband is at work. The moral tone of the Tredwell home is lower than we thought."

Jessica frowned. "That's all true enough, but it's really none of our affair." She smiled. "Their affairs are their own."

"Yes, I suppose so. But I'd like to know more about Virgil Smith all the same. For instance, what does he really do for a living?"

"Maybe he preys on women."

"He looks like a day laborer."

She said, "Maybe Mrs. Tredwell supports him in secret. He doesn't work anywhere else, does he?"

"Not that I've seen." Ki worried his chin. "Do you suppose he's connected in any way with the bank murders? The Tredwells are the most likely prospects to have had something to do with it. Edwards and Gibbs seem like pillars of the church beside them."

"Well, why not give Jack Coleman a look at Virgil?"

"Excellent idea."

Ki went to see Coleman and asked him to come to a particular saloon. "I want you to look at a man. You might know who he is."

"Do you know the name he's using?"

"Virgil Smith."

"That doesn't mean anything to me. Smith is a very common name . . ."

They went to the saloon Virgil frequented and took chairs in a corner. The hours passed and Virgil did not show up. The bartendeer said he had not been in.

Coleman asked, "Do you know where he lives?"

"Yes. Shall we try it?"

"Let's go."

They went to the rooming house, and the landlady said Virgil and Joe had gone that morning.

Ki asked, "Who's Joe?"

"Well, they didn't look anything alike, but Virgil said Joe was his brother. Maybe a half-brother, huh?"

Coleman asked, "Where did they go?"

She said, "I got no idea, mister."

Chapter 11

After a short time in Alister, Virgil had begun to think seriously about Joanna Tredwell. His main worry was that she could point the finger at him if she had a mind to. She would have to do it without implicating herself, but she might manage it.

What if he wrote her a letter?

He had never written a letter in his life, and he tore up half a dozen starts, but finally he wrote one that said something of what he wanted her to believe. Mostly that he missed her. He wrote that he was forced to hide out for the time being, but he was thinking of her.

And he was. He really did miss her—because the saloon girls he took to bed were about as exciting as eating cold beans from a can. He could not remember one from another, nor did he care to. One even ate crackers while he was atop her, pounding away. Another yawned as he labored between her legs.

Joanna had never done that.

Joanna had moaned and pounded her heels on his back and threshed about, each time making him feel as if they were enjoying something very special. He wanted to feel that again.

She could not answer the letter because he did not put a return address on it. But by now she would know all about the robbery and that he was in possession of a million dollars, part of which was hers. She would damn well listen to what he had to say.

When he told Joel he was thinking of returning to Gunnison, the boy was astonished. "Why the hell you want to go back there?"

"Why not?"

"But we robbed the goddam bank shipment!"

"All right, but who knows it? Who knows it was us? Did you tell somebody?"

"Hell no, Virge." Joel shook his head violently. "Don't say them things. Of course not. It's a secret."

"That's right. It's our secret." Virgil poked him with a stiff finger. "So if you don't tell nobody, no one will know." He gestured. "Get your traps together; we moving out."

Virgil explained to the landlady that they had decided to drift on south to Texas, maybe as far as the Rio Grande. He had spent a lot of time along the river, he said, and had many friends there.

She said that was nice, but she didn't care one way or the other.

It was a long journey back to Gunnison.

When they got out on the prairie, Joel wanted to go by the mines and make sure their secret was well kept, but Virgil said no. He would not allow them to go near the place.

They rode far east and came at last into Gunnison a week later.

They took rooms in a boardinghouse run by Mrs. Catwell and her husband, Herb. "No smoking in the rooms, gents," she said." "Go out on the porch."

Virgil approached the Tredwell house at night, scouting

the area for another watcher and finding none. He entered the stable from the alley when he was positive Homer was away. Joanna was astonished to see him.

"I got your letter, but I didn't think you'd show up so soon."

"I couldn't stay away."

She kissed him. "Where's the money?"

He laughed, holding her tight. "It's in a safe place."

"You've hidden it?"

"Of course. We got to wait till all the fuss dies down. Then we'll go get it, and you 'n me, we're going to have fun. Where you want to go?"

"I always wanted to visit New York City . . ."

"Well, you can do that—"

"How long do we have to wait?"

"A few months," Jesus, she was as bad as Joel. "Just a few months. Like I said, till the fuss dies out. Let's go talk about it in the bedroom."

She was willing and quickly got naked. But after he had prodded her awhile she said, "Why do we have to wait so long? Nobody knows—"

"Because, for crissakes, we don't want to get caught."

"But nobody knows who you are. The newspapers would have printed your picture long ago if they knew."

"That's exactly the way I want it. I don't want them ever to find out. Not ever. Then I won't have to be lookin' over my shoulder the rest of my life."

"How many months?"

"Oh, maybe five."

"That's a long time . . ." She sighed. "We're going to move to Farrington soon, Homer says."

"That don't matter."

"But I still have to stay with him—for five months."

He petted her. "It's just for a little while. Jesus! Put up

87

with him. Damn, the things *I* put up with!" He thought of Joel. "Just you keep thinkin' that it'll all be over pretty soon and we'll be rolling in cash." He kissed her. "But don't say it out loud."

She sighed, "Very well . . ."

But when he was alone, Virgil felt uneasy. Women were curious and problematical; you never knew what one of them would do next.

And he had thought that having a million dollars would change everything for the better. So far it hadn't had a chance. He had the million—and he did not have it. He couldn't put his hands on it, not for a while. And having it had actually made his life more difficult. Also he worried that Joel would open his stupid mouth at the wrong time—and now there was Joanna to concern him. She was almost desperate, he thought, to get away from Homer.

Well, everything would be solved when he dug up the money and lit out.

He often thought of leaving them both behind. He would dig it up and disappear. Of course that posed problems, too—Joel knew where it was. If he suddenly turned up missing, Joel would probably head for the mines at once. Joel was dumb, but not that dumb.

He still had half his thousand left, so he did not have to ask Joanna for money. And she was again providing him entertainment in bed, drumming her little heels on his back again as she moaned and orgasmed. Hell, that alone had been worth the trip.

After several weeks in Gunnison, Virgil decided to change boardinghouses. He could not put his finger on the why of it, but it was a feeling, a hunch. He felt eyes on his back. Of course it was foolishness, he told himself, but the hunch made him increasingly uneasy.

He and Joel moved at night to another rooming house, on the edge of town. This time he gave his name as John Larson and Joel was Joe Biggers.

For a time they both stayed away from the saloons they had frequented. Joel spent much time lying on his bunk. Probably dreaming, Virgil thought, of his share.

And now Virgil found himself constantly watchful; he was nervous and sometimes could not keep food down. He told himself he was worried about going back to prison and being hanged. But that would not happen. He said it over and over, mumbling the words aloud.

But of course the law would investigate the crimes he and Joel had committed, and might not let up for years. After all, they had killed four men. It had been a massacre. The law would not soon forget it.

He was watchful because the law might be closing in on him. He did not see how it could—but it was possible. That thought led him to worry more about Joanna. Her husband, Homer, was one of the bank officers. Virgil was positive all the bank people would be carefully investigated, including their husbands and wives.

Joanna would be asked questions. Could he depend on her to send the questioners away satisfied without giving anything away? But what if they became suspicious of her? That might lead them to him.

What should he do? His inclination was not to see her again for a while. She would object, he thought, if only to keep him in view. She did not know where the money was hidden. Certainly the million dollars was always on their minds, hers and Joel's. When he looked at Joel he could almost see it reflected in his eyes. Both of them would want to keep him in view.

But she thought he was the only one who knew. He had not told her about Joel.

He ought to stay away, but he could not, not while he was so close. She excited him too much.

Neither Jessica nor Ki was much disturbed by the disappearance of Virgil Smith from the rooming house. He was probably only a drifter who had attracted Joanna Tredwell by his physical attributes. Such things happened. Possibly they had had a spat and he had left town.

The Tredwells never had visitors, so surveillance on the house was not necessary. Homer continued to call on Lucille at the Red Slipper, going there once or twice every week. It was apparently his only extravagance. As far as could be learned, he had very little money in his bank account.

Two other shipments had gone to Farrington without incident. The secrecy had been impressive, and now most of the papers, documents and other bank property had been transferred. J. M. Thompson was about to announce the bank closing.

Then Ki, checking on the Tredwell house late at night, expecting nothing, a routine check at long intervals, saw Virgil Smith come out of the house and hurry away.

He followed the man to a rooming house on the edge of town. So, he had merely changed addresses. Why would he do that? Was it possible he was wanted by the law for some crime or other?

Curious about Smith, Ki began watching the house. He followed Virgil to a saloon not far away and learned that he was a regular and often came in with his younger brother.

Ki then asked Jack Coleman to come and have a look at Virgil.

In that manner, Jack Coleman was lounging in the saloon one afternoon when Virgil showed up. Coleman took one look and sauntered out.

He said to Ki, "That's Virgil Ropes. He's got a record as long as your left leg."

"Can you arrest him?"

Coleman shook his head. "I got no reason to. He's got a record, but as far as I know, he's not wanted for anything. I got no paper on him. Why are you interested?"

"Because he and his younger brother could be the two who robbed the bank shipment and killed those four men."

"Who is his brother?"

"His name is Joe. He lives at the same rooming house." They rode by and Ki pointed out the house. Jack Coleman then went inside to ask about a fictitious person. He met Ki again at his office.

"I saw the so-called brother. He's Joel Dewey, and not wanted at the moment either. He's a small-time crook. I agree them two could have pulled that holdup, with Virgil the boss."

Ki smiled. "We're making progress."

"Yes, but what the hell're they doing here in town if they did it?"

"Virgil is seeing Joanna Tredwell."

"Jesus!" Jack said.

"Listen, maybe we can search Virgil's room. Do you think you can do that? There might be something . . ."

"Yes, leave that to me."

Ki filled Jessica in on what he had been doing, and she was surprised. "And we thought Virgil was a harmless drifter!"

"Jack says he's served several years in prison for cattle stealing and armed robbery. He's considered one of the dangerous ones."

"And ruthless." She pursed her lips. "I wonder if Joanna knows all this about him?"

"I wonder if she's in it with him."

Jessie nodded. "It's the ideal path for Virgil—he gets information from her and she gets it from Homer."

"Do you think Homer is in it with them? I suspect he isn't. Would he allow Virgil to bed his wife if he were part of it?"

"Probably not. But we're sure Virgil is her lover, aren't we?"

"Yes. So somehow they got information out of Homer—maybe just a hint that he dropped to Joanna, not suspecting she would pass it on. How does that sound?"

Jessie smiled. "I like it fine. Homer learned something at the bank—maybe he stumbled onto something or saw something, and mentioned it over breakfast."

"And she passed it on to her lover. That makes her just as guilty as Virgil and Joel." Ki rubbed his chin. "But we can't prove anything. We've built this case out of thin air, almost—we can't prove a thing. Jack Coleman is going to search Virgil's room, so maybe he'll find something incriminating."

"He wouldn't leave a map there, would he?"

Ki laughed. "Wouldn't that be nice to find! A map to a million dollars!"

"Impossible," Jessie said. "Coleman won't find anything there."

"I'm afraid you're right."

"They can't have all that gold and money in a boarding-house, so it's hidden somewhere and the route to it is in their heads."

Ki sighed. "Yes."

"If it's them," she said.

★

Chapter 12

Marshal Jack Coleman was due to make his monthly report
to the merchants association and so turned over the job
of searching the boardinghouse room to his deputy, Carl
Webber.

Webber was a young man, thirty-four, very bright and
good-looking, and when he met with Jessica and Ki he was
struck by her beauty. Having heard about her exploits, he
expected to see a stringy, tough female who chewed tobacco
and swore like a wagon master.

She and Ki told him what they hoped to find: something
that pertained to the bank; something, anything, that would
connect to the robbery and killings.

They had to wait until both Virgil and Joel were out of
the house, then Webber went inside.

He was gone an hour, and when he came out, he had
found nothing that could be used. "I went through that room
and looked at everything. But they've got no letters, no
notebooks, nothing written down. I could find nothing with
the bank's name on it."

"Well," Ki said. "He's not stupid anyway."

Webber said, "You think Virgil is the brains of that com-
bine?"

"Yes. Probably."

"Then maybe we can get Joel alone." Webber grinned at Jessie. "Give me five minutes. I'll shake something out of him."

"Yes, and warn Virgil we're chasing him." She shook her head. "We're not ready for that yet."

"I like the idea of talking to Joel alone," Ki said. "What if I buy him a few drinks?"

"Isn't he always with Virgil?"

Webber smiled at them. "I'm a deputy marshal. I can take Virgil aside and talk to him about a horse somebody stole . . . or anything else I make up. I'll just ask him if he can help—as an honest citizen doing his civic duty."

Jessica smiled at him and grasped his hand. "That's marvelous. Exactly what we need."

Ki agreed.

They had learned that Virgil was calling himself John Larson, and Joel was using the name Joe Biggers. The next time the two went to the saloon, Carl Webber entered and went to Virgil.

"Excuse me, Mr. Larson . . . I've got a passel of horses I wish you'd look at for us."

"What?" Virgil glanced at the badge, and his face tightened.

Webber smiled. "Nothing to do with you, Mr. Larson. But we been asking the folks at the boardinghouse. All's I want is for you to point out a horse if you can."

"That's all you want?"

"That's it."

"You want Joe here t'go along?"

"No. That isn't necessary. We don't want t'bother you any more'n we have to."

That seemed to mollify Virgil. He got up and nodded. He

gave Joel a look and went out with the deputy. Ki passed them coming into the saloon.

Standing next to Joel at the bar, Ki spilled a handful of coins on the polished surface. He grinned broadly at Joel. "Came into some cash, friend. Have a drink on me."

Joel smiled. "Don't mind iffen I do."

They took a bottle to a table, and Ki talked constantly about nothing, then asked a few questions and talked again, seemingly a harmless, friendly citizen.

Then he happened to say he was waiting for a certain woman—and Joel, not entirely sober by then, said he was waiting for something, too.

"Who you waiting for?" Ki asked.

Joel waved his hand. "Not who . . . waitin' for something."

Ki shook his head miserably. "Waiting is terrible. What you waitin' for?"

"Waitin' for six—" He stopped, looked at the drink in his fist and downed it.

"Six people?" Ki said.

Joel shook his head. "Virge said to—" He stopped again, looked blearily at Ki and pushed his chair back.

"Have a drink," Ki said. "Tomorrow's my birthday." He shook the bottle.

Joel got up unsteadily. "Lemme 'lone." He took a fix on the door, walked to it in a weaving pattern and pushed through.

Ki swore under his breath. What the hell had he meant by six? Six what?

He rejoined Jessie and Webber at the deputy's office and related what had occurred.

Jessie said, "Six months maybe?"

"That makes sense," Webber said. "They're waiting for six months to go by."

Ki nodded. "It could be. They've hidden the bank gold and will go back to get it in six months." He sighed. "That's all supposition, of course. Maybe Virgil is going to get married in six months."

Jessie laughed. "And Joanna Tredwell will be a bridesmaid. I would like to attend that wedding."

The next morning they had a short meeting with J. M. Thompson in his office and reported what they had learned. They were certain Virgil and Joel were the killers who had robbed the bank shipment.

Jessie said, "We think they've hidden the money and are going back for it in six months—probably five months now."

Thompson was angry. He paced the office, chewing on a cigar. "We ought to arrest them—make them talk!"

"What if we're wrong? They could sue you."

He paused and stared at them. "Do you think you could be wrong?"

"Of course, it's possible." Ki glanced at Jessie. "But in this case we don't think so. We've turned up no other suspects. We think we'll have more evidence when we watch these two—"

"Watch them, hell!" Thompson pounded his desk. "They're killers! And they've got the bloody nerve to be living right here in town!"

"Let us—"

"I'll take care of this. I'm going to put those two in jail today!"

"Wait a minute—"

Thompson shooed them out of the office. "I'll handle this now. You go back to the hotel." He shut the door.

They stared at each other.

Jessie said, "I think he just lost the case."

★

Chapter 13

Marshal Jack Coleman was called to the bank for a short meeting with J. M. Thompson, who demanded that Virgil Ropes and young Joel Dewey be immediately arrested and charged with murder and robbery.

Coleman protested that he had no evidence, but he was overruled. Thompson made it clear that Coleman would make the arrests or lose his job.

Thereupon Coleman returned to his office and called in his deputy, Carl Webber. "Get some men together and go get Virgil Ropes and Joel Dewey. They're charged with murder and robbery by J. M. Thompson."

"Thompson has evidence?"

"Hell no. He has a God-given right. He doesn't need evidence. That's for fools like us."

Webber got four men to go along as posse. They rode to the boardinghouse and surrounded it, and Webber went inside. But Virgil and Dewey had flown the coop.

"They left last night," the landlady said.

Webber called the men together and they rode to the outskirts, asking people if they had seen two men in a hurry last night. Several had, and pointed out the direction.

About noon they sighted the pair on the plains. But the

two men saw them as well and took off fast, each in a different direction. Webber swore, divided his force in a hurry and with two men followed the one he thought was Virgil.

He had no jurisdiction out here on the flats, but Marshal Coleman had said, "Bring them in."

However, he lost Virgil that night.

Neither he nor either of his men were trackers. In the morning they found evidence of Virgil's passing, but in a few hours Webber knew they were wasting their time. He called off the search. Virgil could have gone in any direction and they wouldn't know it.

They returned to town to find the other men had had no better luck following Dewey.

Coleman growled, "Those two couldn't have known we were coming after them—they just playing in dumb luck."

He was forced to report to Thompson that the quarry had escaped, left the boardinghouse before the law reached it.

"They got the wind up, JM. Them two is pretty slippery hombres."

Thompson swore. "Then get on the goddam wire and offer a reward. Make it two thousand dollars, dammit! Dead or alive!"

"Not dead, JM! We kill them, where's the money?"

Thompson glared at him, then growled, "All right, dammit, alive. Not a damn nickel if they're dead!"

Carl Webber looked up Jessica, telling her what they had done and what Thompson had ordered.

"Now Virgil knows for sure we suspect him and Joel, and he's going to be hard as hell to locate."

"Yes, and if we're right about that six months business, he could go anywhere and come back when people have forgotten it and him—and pick up his money."

"You can't tell that to a hardhead like Thompson."

She sighed.

When she met Ki in his hotel room later, he worried that they'd lost the case. "Thompson's act has flushed out Virgil into the open, and we may never get on his trail again. And I suppose he doesn't realize it."

"He doesn't listen."

Next Thompson announced that as bank president, he had made a decision to move the bank to Farrington, a hundred miles away. It caused a storm of protest.

The weekly put out a special edition with a black-lined editorial on the front page that did not picture Thompson in a favorable light. He was probably the most hated man in the territory.

But the bank furniture and other property were packed into wagons, and Harrison Edwards went with them on the long trip.

Homer Tredwell went along as well, to find a house, leaving Joanna to put their house up for sale. She promised she would, but she did not. One of these days soon she was going away with Virgil and they would be rolling in wealth. What did she care about the house?

However, she had not seen Virgil for more than a week and was worried. She could not ask about him, so it was doubly annoying. But the local weekly had published an item about him, Virgil Ropes, with a lesser story about young Joel Dewey.

Virgil, according to the paper, was a known criminal and had been incarcerated for twelve years in prison for armed robbery, suspected of murder, and was now wanted for the Gunnison bank robbery and four murders, as was Joel Dewey.

The paper also printed an old prison picture of Virgil

that, she thought, looked nothing much like him.

But it was the only news she had of him. The newspaper said what she already knew: He had dropped out of sight. Of course, he had done that before and had come back. He had to come back, to take her away so they could enjoy the stolen riches.

She spent endless hours wondering about him. It was terrible that the law now knew his name. It made it so much more difficult for him. He had hoped they would never find out.

Jack Coleman duly sent out requests for information about Virgil. prison authorities were asked to provide what facts they knew, and in due course some responded.

Virgil had been put into the same cell for several years with a man named Floyd Hicks, a robber and suspected killer. Hicks was now out on parole. His home was in Oklahoma Territory, and it was supposed he would go there when released. A warden suggested that Virgil would look him up.

Jessie and Ki thought it a very good suggestion. Virgil was an orphan, so prison records said. He had no particular home and no kinfolk.

They read the reports and agreed with the warden. Virgil might very well go to Oklahoma Territory, not only to see his old pal, Hicks, but because the territory was poorly policed and sparsely settled. A man might hide out there forever.

It was only a small step from reading to deciding. Jessie said, "Let's go see Hicks."

Their information said the Hicks family lived in a tiny little burg named Holman, not even a dot on the map. The stage would take them within seventy miles of the town. They would have to buy horses and ride the rest of the distance. The houses in the town had no addresses, they were told. They would have to ask for Hicks.

They had to wait a day for the stage, then make a transfer en route. It took them six days to get to the town of Joris, seventy miles from Holman. And when they got down from the stagecoach they felt battered.

Joris was a bustling county seat, so they put up at the best hotel and slept the clock round. When they had risen and had breakfast, Ki went out and purchased two roan horses. Jessie picked out a saddle, and in an hour they were outfitted and ready.

The stableman drew a crude map for them. Holman was south and east, he said. "Follow the river for about ten miles. It'll cut west and you go on straight. You'll see hills in the distance. Holman is just the other side of 'em."

There was no road. They came to the river in several miles and followed it as the man had said. Along the river was a path of sorts, but when the river curved west, the path did also.

They continued southeast and in several hours saw the faint blurs of the hills. After several hours riding in the morning, the hills became more distinct. By evening they were close, and Jessie and Ki made camp in a narrow canyon where a spring filled a large pond.

They came to the town the next day, and it was as small as they had been told, barely a wide place in the road, with no apparent reason for being. The grocery owner told them the town served the ranchers and was hanging on by its toenails.

He knew the Hicks family well. They lived at the end of the road. He went out to the street with them and pointed.

Yes, he knew Floyd Hicks. "He was a hellion, Floyd was, till he up and left. We heard he was in jail . . . not surprised."

"Have you seen him lately?"

103

The older man shook his head. "Nope," He looked at them sharply. "You two after him?"

"No. He's a friend of someone else . . ."

They thanked the man and stayed in town in one of the two saloons. It would hardly do to ride up to the house if Floyd and Virgil were inside. It might even be fatal.

That night they looked the house over. It was a weathered frame building with a fieldstone chimney. There was a small stable in the back and a corral with two mules inside and a wagon parked beside it.

Ki slipped up close to the house and peered in the windows. There was a very old man and a ragged woman, but no Virgil or Floyd. The house had only three rooms and he could see into two. He remained by the window for an hour, but no one came out of the third room.

He returned to Jessica, shaking his head. "I don't think they're here in town."

She said, "Horses in the stable?"

"No."

"Then maybe they were here and have gone . . ."

"Yes. Damn."

The guesses of the prison authorities were quite right. Floyd Hicks had gone directly home on being released. They had given him ten dollars, some clean clothes, not new, and nothing else but a ticket on the Winfield and Southern Railway. It would take him to Prescott, a town perhaps fifty miles from home.

How he managed that last fifty miles was his affair. The state had washed its hands with the ticket.

So, in Prescott, Floyd had had a few beers, waited for nightfall and stolen a mule. He rode the fifty miles and, when he arrived in Holman, put the mule in someone else's corral. Let them argue with the law.

But home was just as dreary and run-down as he'd left it. Maybe a little more cheerless and depressing . . . The town was dying; there wasn't a woman in it less than seventy. No whores at all and nothing to do but play solitaire or a little poker with one or two of the old-timers who were so slow and crotchety he could stand them for only a short time.

And then Virgil showed up.

Virgil came riding into town one afternoon late, with a kid named Joel Dewey. Floyd happened to be sitting on the porch, feet up on the rail, wondering what the hell he was doing there.

When he saw Virgil he hardly believed his eyes. He gave a whoop and ran out to the dusty street as Virgil slid down. They yelled and slapped each other.

"Where the hell did you drop from, you old son of a bitch!"

"We come from over north. Who let you out of jail?"

"They give up on me. I'm too tough."

"Yeah, all tough and no brains."

"Who's the kid with you?"

Virgil said, "That's Joel Dewey. Shake with Floyd Hicks, Joe."

They said howdys, and Floyd suggested they go to the town's only saloon.

"Sure."

They went down the street and into the deadfall. Floyd ordered beer.

Virgil paid for a pitcher and they took it to a table.

Floyd laughed. "It's like old times. You got any money, Virge?"

"No. That's like old times, too. I got a couple hundred dollars, but that ain't money."

"We got to get us some kale and get the hell out'n this

place. I been cooped up too goddam long." Floyd poured into their glasses and glanced around. No one was near. "We can make us a pile over in Underhill."

Virgil was interested. "You got something figgered?"

"Damn right."

"Not a bank? I d'want to go up agin any of them shotgun guards."

"No, not a bank. This feller is a horse and cattle buyer. Buys and sells 'em. You know a herd is big money, cows sellin' for maybe fifteen dollars a head."

"You got a bead on this hombre?"

Floyd nodded. "I watched 'im two, three days. Allus does the same thing. And a straight line out of town into the woods. No goddam thing to it. It's a lead-pipe cinch."

"How much money you think?"

"At least five thousand. That'll show us a good time, huh, Virge?"

They didn't consult Joel. Virgil said, "All right. Let's go look at this cow buyer."

Floyd didn't own a horse. There was a saddle hanging in the stable at home. It wasn't much, but it would do. Virgil and Joel put up the money for the horse—Floyd would pay them back when they had done the job. They rode out for Underhill and entered the town after dark.

Each of them rented a room in a different rooming house, and they met next day at the Good Night Saloon.

The proposed victim's name, Floyd told them, was Judson Rails. He drew a little sketch on a scrap of paper. "This here's his office. There's a safe inside that he keeps open during the day. It's a frame building with a sort of porch and a couple steps up."

"Anybody with him in the office?"

"I seen a woman there once. Maybe she was a clerk or something. There wasn't no man around. The office is on

106

a side street around the corner from the bank. Rails goes to the bank every morning and sometimes in the afternoon."

He took them to look it over. They rode past at a walk and Virgil studied the building. It was exactly as Floyd had said. A one-room building with some other closed buildings on either side. They'd give no trouble. Rails had a buggy at the side of the building.

They rode to the edge of town, and it was a straight shot, as Floyd had said, across some grassy lots to the fields and across them to the woods. They could be in the woods in five minutes. The woods were ten or fifteen miles deep.

They returned to the saloon. "I seen him come from the bank," Floyd said. "He got a brown carpetbag he carries. I seen him put money from the bank in the safe."

"How'd you get close enough to see that?"

"Didn't get close. I had a spyglass."

Virgil said, "He'd only get money from the bank when he was buyin' some cows, huh? How d'we know when he does that?"

"When he got men in the office. Then he goes down to the corrals by the siding. After that they go back to the office and Rails pays over the cash. I watched 'em do it."

Virgil nodded. That made sense. "All right, then we got to set watches on him. They's three of us, so it ought t'be easy. We'll start tomorra."

It was no trouble to watch the office. They could do it from a block away. They took turns, two hours a turn. It was monotonous work, but it had to be done.

The second day they watched, three men entered the office, getting out of a heavy buggy. Joel was on watch and he alerted the others at once. They followed the four men to the corrals and waited as the buyers and sellers talked and spit and talked some more, and finally shook hands.

They drove back to the office and Rails got out. The others went on.

The next morning when the bank opened, Rails went there with his brown carpetbag.

Floyd said, "When he comes back, Virge and I go into the office. Joe stands guard outside with our horses."

"And no shooting," Virgil said. "No noise at all."

"No need to," Floyd said.

"Good." Virgil nudged Floyd. "Here he comes."

They watched Rails go up the steps and into the office.

"Let's go," Floyd said.

★

Chapter 14

With a last look around, Virgil stepped up on the porch. The board creaked.

Inside the office Rails closed the door of the safe and spun the wheel, locking it. As he turned, he slipped a revolver from his belt. He had been robbed once before and was taking no chances. He saw two strangers with pistols in their hands—and he fired.

Virgil jerked in surprise, then fired three times at point-blank range. Rails hit the floor, and the revolver bounced away and thudded against the far wall.

Virgil said, "Shit!" He was hit. It had felt like a punch in the belly. He went to his knees, and he thought of Joanna as he dropped his gun. He reached for the floor and Floyd's hands were on him and he heard the other's voice from a long way off . . .

Floyd let him down easy and stared at him. There was blood everywhere. He turned as Joel yelled from the door, "What happened?"

"Virge's shot bad—looks bad as hell." Floyd felt for a pulse, and Joel came in and tried the safe door.

"Damn thing's locked!"

He turned Rails over. "This one's dead."

109

"I think Virge is, too. He ain't got a pulse."

They both knelt over him, and Joel said, "Shit. Now what?"

Floyd turned out Rails's pockets and found twenty dollars. "We got to get outa here." Floyd was suddenly galvanized. He pocketed the money. "Somebody musta heard that shootin'. Come on." He ran out to the horses.

They left Virge's horse behind and loped down the street, then spurred across lots as they had planned. They saw no one but a stout woman with a white cat. She gazed at them, shading her eyes. Then they were in the grassy field, pounding toward the dark green woods.

Floyd led the way, straight east, letting the horse run. Jesus! Virge was dead! It was hard to get used to. He reined in after about twenty minutes. "I think we got away all right . . ."

Joel said, "That goddam safe was locked!"

"He locked it when he heard us on the porch. We didn't figger that. Then he shot Virge. They both fired at the same time."

"And killed each other . . ." Joel let out his breath, feeling miserable.

"Let's get going . . ."

"Damn," Joel said, "it ain't going to be the same without Virge."

He followed Floyd along a grassy path through the trees, and it didn't occur to him about the money for a long time. Then it hit him—now it was all his! He almost yelped out in his excitement, but managed to hold it in. It was all his! He was the only one in the world who knew where it was! He grinned at Floyd's back. He was rich and he didn't have to divvy with anyone!

And he didn't have to wait Virgil's damn six months now. He could go back and get some of it anytime he wanted.

And now was the time to do what Virgil had said. Keep your mouth shut!"

He didn't trust Floyd—but of course Floyd thought he had nothing, so that didn't figure. If Floyd knew about the money in the mine! Jesus! Floyd would shoot him at the first chance.

He let Floyd do the leading. They stopped for the night in some forested hills, and Floyd was in a bad mood. "We didn't get no money and we lost Virge. Dammit, that's a goddam poor swap."

"You got any money at all?"

Floyd sighed deeply. "Got a couple dollars." He pulled it out to show. Joel emptied his pockets. He had a little less than eighty dollars. "We ain't broke . . ."

"Damn near. We got to get us some kale. Next town we come to, we'll look around."

The next big town was Hendry, and it took them nearly a week to reach it. A local paper was just out and they read it sitting in a saloon. It said that three men had tried to hold up Judson Rails, cattle buyer, in the town of Underhill. Rails and one of the would-be robbers were killed. The dead man was identified as Virgil Ropes, a man with a long criminal record. There was a photo of Virgil, a very poor reproduction.

The item went on to say that Rails had just withdrawn thirty thousand dollars from the local bank that morning. He had apparently locked it in the safe moments before he was shot. The money was still in the safe when his widow opened it later.

Floyd and Joel moaned, reading the paper. They had barely missed a fortune!

A woman had told the authorities she had seen two men galloping away. A horse had been found at the scene, so it was assumed that three men had come to rob Rails.

The other two were unidentified.

Hendry had a hotel, seven rooms, at seventy-five cents a night. That, and what they had to spend to eat, and they would be broke soon. They looked over the only bank in town. There was a shotgun guard behind the teller's cage.

Floyd said, "Shotguns makes me nervous as hell."

They watched the stage handlers heave up a heavy cash box onto the coach and shove it under the seat. Then a big competent-looking shotgun guard climbed up and settled himself. They wandered on.

"Honest folks don't trust nobody," Floyd grumbled.

They found some empty chairs along the street and sat to figure what to do next. Horsemen went by and wagons rattled along the rutted street. As it grew dark a merchant across the street came out, slammed the door closed and locked it, then shook the knob. He carried a fat black bag. They watched him go around the side of the building and climb the stairs. In a few moments a light went on in the rooms over the store.

Joel said, "What he got in the bag?"

"What he took in today." Floyd looked at Joel and grinned. "I think we just got our meal ticket."

Jack Coleman and Carl Webber talked it over. They knew that Virgil Ropes was seeing Joanna constantly. Was she implicated in the robbery-murders? Virgil had disappeared, but maybe she knew where he'd gone. Jack decided to bring her in for questioning.

Webber went to the house with a buggy and asked her to come to the jail office. She was indignant, "What for?"

"The marshal wants t'ask you about Virgil Ropes, ma'am." He could see that she wanted to deny she knew Virgil, but there was indecision in her eyes. How much did the law really know? In the end, she went with him.

112

Jessica and Ki listened to the questioning. She was defensive, sitting upright, hands clutching a handkerchief in her lap, staring at Coleman. No, she had no idea where Virgil was now. She knew him only slightly.

He said, "You were seen kissing him."

That startled her. How could anyone see inside her house? Coleman did not press it.

"Did you ever discuss the bank holdup with him?"

"No. Never. I knew nothing to discuss."

"Did you know he was a criminal with a record?"

"No. Certainly not."

"How did you meet him?"

"I hired him to paint our stable."

"Painting the stable was finished some long time ago, yet he still visited your home daily."

She firmed her lips, saying nothing.

Coleman persisted. "You say you know nothing at all about the bank holdup?"

"Nothing."

"We know that Virgil did it, killing four men."

She looked into her lap.

"Do you realize, Mrs. Tredwell, that if it is proved that you helped Virgil you are guilty as well?"

She stared at him, and the color seemed to drain from her face. Her eyes fluttered and she suddenly wilted. Carl Webber jumped to grab her from falling.

"Jesus, she fainted!"

"Take her in and lay her on one of the cots," Coleman said. He opened the door to the jail cells. Webber carried her in.

"She helped Virgil," Jessie said. "She's scared to death."

"I'm going to hold her on suspicion," Coleman said. "Where the hell you s'pose Virgil got to?"

They shook their heads. That night they heard the story

113

as it came over the wire. Virgil had been killed in Underhill trying to rob a cattle buyer who was also killed. There had been two men with Virgil, both unidentified, though one was thought to be Joel Dewey and the other might be Floyd Hicks.

Webber said, "Why was he trying to rob someone if he had a million dollars from the bank?"

"Because the million is stashed away," Jessie said.

Ki agreed. "He and the others have to pay daily expenses. And there's one good thing about it . . ."

"What?" Coleman demanded.

Ki smiled at him. "It means the stash is still hidden, intact. Or they wouldn't need to rob someone."

"That's right," Webber said, grinning at Jessie.

Joel and Floyd went back to the saloon to plan the next move. "We wait for him to come out of the store . . ."

Floyd said, "Why? Why not go in the store just before he locks up for the night? That way we can go out the back instead of the street."

Joel nodded. "All right. Then nobody will see us climbing them stairs."

"Then we do it tomorrow night . . ."

Joel nodded. "Let's have another beer."

There was no alley behind the merchant's store, there was only a brown field that stretched away to the hills. Backed up to the store building was a line of sheds with heavy padlocks. There were rows of trash barrels and boxes and an incinerator outside the sheds, with some privies as well. All the stores had rear doors, some had hitch racks and one had a roofed passageway to the privy.

The store owner had locked his door at approximately five o'clock the day before, probably his usual time of closing.

Joel tied their horses behind the store at a quarter of five and followed Floyd around to the front.

The big black-and-white sign on the store read; Hats, Caps & Boots, Jeremiah Posy, Prop. When Floyd opened the door, a bell tinkled. The store smelled strongly of leather, and the same man they'd seen the night before was behind a short counter at the rear, putting something into the same black bag.

He looked up as the bell sounded, and slid the bag under the counter. "Howdy, gents."

"How do," Floyd said, smiling broadly. He walked to the counter and drew his pistol. "Don't put your hands up—move over there." He motioned aside with the gun barrel.

"Goddam!" the man said. "You—"

"Shut up." Floyd pulled the hammer back, and the man took a quick breath, moving as Floyd had ordered.

Joel hurried around the counter and pulled the black bag out. It contained bills and coins. There was also money in a small wooden box, and he quickly dumped it into the bag. The man watched him, scowling, gritting his teeth.

Joel said, "That's it."

Floyd pushed the man through a black curtain into the back of the store. "Sit down."

The man sat on a straight chair, and Joel wound a length of cord around his wrists behind his back and tied it. Then he tied the man's ankles together as Floyd went out to the front and locked the door from the inside.

Then Joel tied the man to the chair. "You ain't gonna get away with this . . ." the man said.

"'Course not," Floyd said. He pushed Joel toward the rear door. "Let's go."

They went out slowly, Joel with the bag, looking around, but no one was behind the stores. They mounted the horses

· 115

and rode across the brown field, directly away from the store, heading west.

A half mile away, Floyd looked back; no one followed them. It would probably take the owner a while to get out of his bindings, unless someone came into the rear of the store and found him.

It was getting dark by the time they reached the first low hills. They halted while it was still light and dumped the bag out onto a flat rock. Floyd counted the contents quickly as Joel bit his lips. They had two hundred and eleven dollars and about three dollars in coins.

"You got it all?" Floyd demanded.

"Yeah, I got ever' bit that was in the box."

"Damn. It's not very much."

"Jesus, it's better'n nothing at all, Floyd."

Floyd divided it grumpily and tossed the bag away.

★

Chapter 15

His wife in jail!? Homer Tredwell was astonished. He hurried there and talked to Marshal Jack Coleman. "What the hell, Jack?"

Coleman quickly filled him in on what they knew and suspected.

Homer listened, face sagging. "Are you saying she was seeing this Virgil every day—in my house?"

"In your bed, I'm afraid."

Homer sat down and closed his eyes. The perfidy of women! It took a few moments for him to remember—she had asked him repeatedly about when the shipments would move to Farrington. So that's why she was so concerned—she was part of the robbery!

He also knew he must not tell them about that. It would involve *him*.

He kept shaking his head in disbelief. Joanna had a man in her bed—their bed—every day! And he had never suspected a thing. He said to Coleman, "I remember now—she asked me if she could hire a man to paint the stable . . ."

"That was the man."

Homer could not believe it. "She picked a perfect stranger

to go to bed with? The first man who came along—a workman who painted the stable!"

Coleman said, "Of course we don't know how long she knew him. She won't tell us much. D'you want to talk to her?"

"No. Hell no. I don't want to see her."

"We think she knows more than she's telling."

Tredwell shook his head. He waved Coleman off. "I will not see her. Keep her in the goddam jail for the rest of her life." He stared at the lawman. "You think she knows where the money is?"

Jack Coleman shrugged. "Maybe not . . ."

Homer took a deep breath. "What about that other one— what was his name?"

"Joel Dewey. He wasn't involved with your wife, as far as we know. Only Virgil." The marshal scratched a match and lit a cigar. "So will you get her bail?"

"Hell no. I will not."

Homer stalked out of the jail office. He walked several blocks, hands in his pockets. Joanna in bed with a criminal . . . Jesus Christ! What women did when they went bad!

He shook his head and went to see Lucille.

Jessica and Ki took the stage to Underhill and talked to Sheriff Ben Elsby. He was a big, solid citizen with a gray mustache and wrinkled clothes.

"I formed a posse and went after them two, but they lost us. They had an hour start. We never did catch up to them."

"Can you be sure who they were?"

Elsby shook his head. "We can be pretty damn sure one of 'em was Joe Dewey. They was runnin' together, him and Virgil. We know that Floyd Hicks got out of prison and went home, and we's pretty sure Virgil and Dewey went to see him. Holman ain't a very big place—that's where Hicks lived—and we got descriptions of Virgil and Joe Dewey bein' there."

"That tallies with what we know, Sheriff."

Ki asked, "Was there anything on Virgil's body that might give a clue about the money?"

"Not a thing. No letters, no writin' at all. He had about forty dollars in his pants. We buried him over 'crost the tracks. Nobody come to the funeral. The forty paid for a good box and a headboard."

"And that's it . . ."

"Well, we wired surroundin' towns to keep a lookout for 'em. But nothing turned up."

They thanked Elsby and left.

Ki said, "Has Joel Dewey told Floyd about the money?"

"A very interesting question. From all we've heard, Joel is not a college graduate."

Despite all he'd said to Jack Coleman, Homer Tredwell returned to the jail and demanded to see his wife.

Coleman shrugged and unlocked the door.

There were four cells in the little jail. Joanna was the only prisoner. She was lying on a bunk, eyes closed, and he thought she was sleeping.

He kicked the bars, and she opened her eyes and looked at him.

He said, "So you got yourself in jail!"

"Go away."

"Did you have to go to bed with him in my house?"

She turned her face away.

He kicked the bars again. "Dammit, Joanna! What got into you? What made you take up with that man?"

"For God's sake, Homer, go away."

He yelled at her, but she refused to say another word. Finally he gave up and went back into the office. Reluctantly he handed over the bail money.

"I'm going home and pack," he told Coleman. "I'll be taking the next stage to Farrington. Don't let her out for a couple of hours."

"All right, Homer."

Joanna was surprised when Marshal Coleman unlocked the cell door. "You can go now, Miz Tredwell." She slid off the bunk, and he warned, "But stay in town."

"I'm going to put the house up for sale, Marshal. Then I want to go home to Maryland."

"Can't let you do that."

"Why not?"

"Because if there's a trial, you gonna be in it."

"But I had nothing to do with stealing that money! Virgil did it all! I don't know where the money is any more than you do."

Coleman shook his head. "If you try t'leave town, Miz Tredwell, I'll have to put you back in here." He cocked his head at her. "You want to gimmie your word?"

"Oh, all right . . ."

The marshal watched her leave and fished for a fresh cigar. He said to Carl Webber, "She knows more'n she's tellin' us."

"You really think she knows where the money is?"

Coleman looked at him. "You know—I *hope* she does."

"You do? Why?"

"Because—if she doesn't know, then it looks t'me like there's only one person who does, and that's Joe Dewey. And Dewey is too goddam dumb to know a thing like that."

Webber laughed. "You got a point, Jack."

"So we'll keep a watch on her."

• • •

Jessica and Ki returned from Underhill, both feeling frustrated. They had learned very little. They were fairly sure, they told the marshal, that Floyd Hicks and Joel Dewey were together, now that Virgil was dead, but it was anyone's guess how long they would stay together.

Coleman said that separate posters were being printed. They would be distributed to every town within two hundred miles.

Carl Webber went to the hotel with them and had supper with Jessica while Ki went up to his room.

She said, "There's not much chance of finding Joel Dewey with a poster, is there?"

"No. Not much. We don't have a picture of him yet, for one thing. We do have a prison photograph of Floyd . . ." He made a face. "Of course, he'll change his appearance."

"You think that Joel will tell Hicks, don't you?"

"I think that if Floyd knows or realizes that Joe knows about the money, he'll wring it out of him, yes."

"I'm afraid you're right." She smiled at him as his hand reached for hers and caressed her slim fingers. Emboldened, he leaned toward her and his lips brushed her cheek. They were in a dim corner of the dining room, and she was greatly tempted to press her mouth to his, but if they were noticed it would cause a stir.

She pinched his thigh. "Not here. There is a Spanish saying, that the walls have ears. They also have eyes. My room is number eleven. Come there in an hour."

He nodded, not trusting himself to speak.

Joel and Floyd Hicks arrived in Benson after dark. It was a small burg far off the railroad and stage line, but as they got down in front of the Gold Dust Saloon, they saw the posters, a line of them on the wall.

121

Theirs were the newest. Both said, WANTED for MURDER, with their names and descriptions. Floyd's poster had a photograph that could have been almost anyone. He stared at it, remembering when it was taken, in the Territorial Prison at Reedsville.

Joel said, "I be piss-damned! They got them up already!"

Floyd glanced around. No one was nearby. "We got to use different names. What you want?"

"I was Joe Biggers once . . ."

"All right. I'll be Johnny Getts. He was with me in the can." He poked a finger. "Don't forget and call me Floyd."

"'Course not. Let's get a drink."

The saloon was quiet: two men playing cards, the bartender half-asleep. He served them beer, and asked for news; they had none, and he went back to dozing.

They sat at a far table, and Joel said, "I think I'm going to hit for Texas."

"Texas!"

"It's a far piece, but I got kinfolk there in Austin. What you going to do?"

"I dunno. But I ain't going to Texas."

Joel sipped the beer, thinking about the money in the mine. No sense in sharing it with Floyd. He hardly knew the man. Actually he knew no one in Texas but had heard Floyd mention one time that he hated Texas. He'd gotten into some kind of trouble there . . .

He was very pleased with himself about deluding Floyd.

The town had one small hotel with rooms the size of shotgun barrels. The proprietor asked fifty cents a night, and the doors didn't even have locks.

They put their horses in the stable behind the building and hit the hay. Their rooms were several doors from each other on the only floor.

Someone was snoring loudly as Joel flopped on the bunk.

122

He stared at the dark ceiling. So far Floyd hadn't found out that he and Virgil were the ones who had done the bank holdup. It had been in the papers, but apparently Floyd wasn't much of a reader. Of course he couldn't depend on that. Sooner or later Floyd would hear it or read it. Then it would occur to him that Joel knew where the money was.

That would be a bad thing for Floyd to know.

Joel lay quiet for more than an hour. Then he got up, took his blanket roll and Winchester and tiptoed out to the back stable. He saddled his horse and rode away quietly, pointing west.

More than a month had passed since they'd put the money in the mine. Virge had said to wait six months at least, but Virgil was the cautious type. Over-cautious.

And he was almost broke. The best thing to do was to go to the mine and collect another thousand dollars—just to see him through the wait. He'd wait a few more months.

He needed money desperately, but he did not want to take a chance on getting shot—like Virgil had been. Virge was rich, but needed ready cash, and look what it got him. A lonely grave.

Joel shook his head. Too damn bad. He wasn't going to wind up that way.

In the morning, when Floyd rolled out, he waited for Joel a few minutes, then rapped on the other's door. No one answered. When he looked inside, Joel was gone.

He went out to the stable. Joel's horse was gone, too. The kid must have slid away in the night. He was sure damn anxious to get to Texas.

Floyd went to have breakfast. It was no skin off his ass. The kid hadn't been that great a traveling companion anyway.

The restaurant was small and steamy. He sat at a counter

with two other gents, who were talking about some holdup or other, one saying he sure would like to have that million dollars. Floyd saw they were talking about an item in the paper spread out between them.

Floyd pricked up his ears at the mention of a million dollars. *Was* there that much money in the world?

He ordered eggs and bacon, and when the two men left the restaurant, leaving the newspaper behind, Floyd pulled it over and read the item.

It was the bank holdup between Farrington and Gunnison. He had heard about it vaguely, of course. He was about to shove the paper away when his eye was caught by a name: Virgil Ropes. He read the paragraph.

It was the first time he knew that Virgil had been the man who had done the killing and robbery. Four men had been shot down. No wonder Virge had been close-mouthed.

He ate the eggs, thinking about it. Virge had showed up at Holman with Joel Dewey. So Joe had been with Virge! The paper said the money had never been recovered.

An icy feeling gripped Floyd's spine. He had been riding with a man who knew where a million dollars was hidden!

★

Chapter 16

Carl Webber lay on the bed naked and watched Jessica come across the room to him, her long blond hair down about her shoulders, breasts bobbing lusciously, a smile on her beautiful face as she crawled onto the bed beside him.

"I think I'm dreaming," he said.

"Why?"

"I don't believe I'm here . . ."

She pinched his erection. "Do you feel that?"

He pulled her close. "How can I believe I'm here on a bed with the most beautiful girl in the territory—in the country!"

"You had better believe it." She fondled the rampant organ, making him squirm. He teased her nipples with his tongue, then took part of a delicious breast into his mouth as she leaned over him, continuing to stroke him . . . .

Then her leg slid across him, and she moved gently, straddling him, smiling down. He cupped her breasts with both hands, feeling his shaft guided—entering her warmly.

She eased herself forward, and the thick erection buried itself as she sighed. Then her inner muscles began working, and he gasped, never having felt such a thing before.

He slid his hands about her, holding her velvety buttocks, feeling them moving sinuously, excitingly. He arched his back, driving his spike upward, and she cooed in pleasure, rubbing her hands over his nipples.

Then he could stand it no longer. He rolled her over onto her back as she laughed and held him tightly. Her legs slid about him, and she pulled him down close as he stroked into her desperately . . .

He lasted only a few minutes, jerking spasmodically, panting as she bit his ear and licked into it.

Then she held him and kissed him, and after a bit the organ revived, as she knew it would, and once more they heaved and rolled, this time lasting much longer . . .

J. M. Thompson kept only one man from the Gunnison Bank, Harrison Edwards, his brother-in-law.

Homer Tredwell received his final notice and had already made arrangements to set up shop as an accountant. He rented a room and went to work with scarcely an interval. Let Joanna do as she pleased. He was through with her forever.

Jerome Gibbs did not move to Farrington. He remained behind, and since he owned a number of properties, he decided merely to collect his rents and live quietly.

Joanna did not attempt to sell the house—where would she live? Jack Coleman would not allow her to go to her parents' home in Maryland . . .

She had read of Virgil's death in Underhill and felt very sorry for him. He had been an outcast and had murdered people, but she still remembered fondly their intimate moments together.

She wished, however, he had told her where the money was hidden.

Jessica and Ki sat in a restaurant as Ki sipped coffee

after the meal. He said, "It's unlikely they brought the bank money into town, wouldn't you think?"

"I thought we agreed on that."

"Yes. I'm sure they hid it out in the sticks, maybe in the hills somewhere."

She nodded. "It would have to be somewhere not affected by rain and changes of season . . . and somewhere no one would stumble over it. What kind of a place would that be?"

"Not a deserted shack. How about a cave?"

"Yes." She tapped the table. "A cave would do very well indeed. The right one, of course."

"But are there caves in this part of the country?"

"We'll have to look at a map."

Jack Coleman supplied the map, the latest one, he told them. Maps were rare items and usually inaccurate.

This one was not much help. They pored over it and marked likely spots, but caves were not labeled. If there were any, they would have to go out and search for them.

They questioned some of the oldest citizens and got ambiguous answers. There used to be caves here and there, but that was a long time ago . . . Things changed.

They asked a bartender if he'd heard talk. He directed them to a cattleman.

The cattleman said, "They some caves along the river, maybe a hunnerd miles south, but I don't remember none big enough for a man to live in. Anyways, when the water rises, it fills the caves."

Ki shook his head. Can't be them, then.

Jessica asked, "What other natural features . . ."

The cattleman said, "What about mines? They lots of mine holes out in the hills."

Jessie smiled at Ki. A mine would do nicely. But their map showed none at all.

They talked to a bartender who said, "There was a gold strike over east a few years back, maybe fifty miles. I never been there, but I heard the gab. It played out pretty quick."

It was their best bet so far. They bought victuals and set out eastward, hoping they weren't on a wild goose chase.

Fifty miles or so brought them to a settlement called Handy's Place. Fred Handy ran the general store and the blacksmith shop. Yes, there was a strike—few years back.

"It was over north a few miles, twenty maybe. But there's no one there now."

"We just go straight north from here?" Jessie asked.

"What you want to go there for anyways?"

"Curiosity," Ki said. "Are there diggings there yet?"

"Sure. But don't you go into any of them holes . . . damn dangerous."

Jessie smiled. "We'll be careful."

"Well, you go north from here. I think the trail is still there, most places."

"Thanks."

"Good luck."

The trail was still visible on the ground. Wheeled vehicles had been that way and had rutted it. They had no trouble following. They had to camp halfway there and came to the end of the road the next day. It was a small valley ringed with test holes. Only a few were deep enough to walk into. There were the remains of shacks and a huge pile of burned trash, cans and bottles . . . But no treasure. They investigated every hole carefully. It had been a long ride for nothing.

Ki prowled over the area where the shacks had stood and dug under where the front doors had been . . . still nothing.

Reluctantly, they turned back.

• • •

Joel Dewey went across country, navigating by the sun, avoiding towns, generally pointing west. The mine where the money was hidden was probably a hundred miles distant—give or take fifty or so.

It had occurred to him a few times that he might not be able to find it if he waited too long. His memory could fade, and the land changed. Trees grew up or floods moved the washes around; the whole appearance of the land could be different.

But he was reasonably sure that if he stuck to the road from Gunnison to Farrington, he would remember where the wagon had turned off. Of course then he hadn't paid much attention . . . that was what worried him most. He had been jittery as hell after the shooting.

He didn't have enough money to buy vittles, to support himself for long while he searched. He was the richest man in the country and nearly flat broke at the same goddam time. It was some joke!

In several days he came across the trading post. He halted, seeing it in the distance, a squarish gray stone building with a log-and-dirt roof, tall with weeds, a corral beside it and a column of dark smoke rising. As he came closer he saw a shed behind the house and a flock of dirty brown tents off to the right, by a creek. Probably Indians.

Joel rode in slowly, eyes everywhere. The crude lettering on a board nailed up over the door read, Gen'l Post, L. Kettleman, Prop.

Joel got down—it all seemed peaceful—and opened the plank door. He was in one large room with a huge black belly stove in the center, the stove pipe rising through the ceiling. There were goods of every kind hung on the walls by the shelves and dangling from the ceiling. The room smelled of leather, grease, tobacco and other, nameless things.

Joel rubbed his nose and someone said, "Howdy, stranger . . ."

A man came around a counter, "What's the news, friend?"

Joel said, "Guess I don't know more'n you do." He gazed around. "I been out in the sticks."

"Then you'll need a bottle." Kettleman set one on the the crowded counter.

Joel shook his head. "Can't afford it. I'm about flat. Could use some beans . . ."

"In a sack or in a can?"

"Can." He wondered if Kettleman had much hard money behind the counter. It might be easy to stick him up.

Then he noticed the face framed in some dress goods. It was a woman with black hair and a grim mouth, staring at him from behind a huge pile. And sticking out just below her chin was a revolver barrel.

Kellerman took no chances.

Joel gave the woman a brief smile. "Howdy, ma'am." He paid for the beans, chatted with the proprietor a moment and went out to the horse. He wondered if the woman shot many pilgrims. She had looked as if it wouldn't bother her much.

Kellerman had said there was a town due west maybe fifty miles. He went that way, intending to stop over, but he missed it. Probably went right past it—which would have been easy to do.

In a day or two he came to a road and followed it, but it petered out finally, leading nowhere. He stopped then and looked at the sky. He was lost.

There was only one thing to do: keep moving west.

In another day he came to Elkton, a bustling little town

130

full of gamblers and whores. It was on the edge of a copper mining area, on a stage line.

Joel slept in a stable, beside his horse, and bought a fifteen-cent breakfast the next morning. He asked the way to Gunnison.

No one in the restaurant had heard of it. Or Farrington either. He went to the stage station, and the ticket seller told him Gunnison was a hundred miles west and north. But his stage line did not go there.

Joel thanked him and went back to the stable to count his remaining cash. A couple dollars. Virgil had said they would have to get jobs when their money ran out. But what could he do? He had no trade . . .

He spent two days sweeping out saloons, but it cost him food and oats for the horse—he could never get ahead on the pennies they paid him.

After working all day he sat in the darkened stable and sniffled. He felt enormously sorry for himself. He was rich, but hungry. He thought about going to someone and selling him a share in the mine . . . No—that would lead to nothing but trouble.

He walked along the back of the line of stores on the main street. He didn't want to go in with a gun and hold up one of the merchants . . . but he might get in a window and find a few dollars . . .

The dry goods store had a promising, low window. It was next to some stairs that went to the second floor, and it was easy to reach.

Joel peered around carefully, looking at every shadow. It was very late and there was no one to be seen. He slipped his coat off, pressed it against the pane of the window and hit it with his elbow.

There was a sharp clatter, and Joel sat motionless for a few minutes, listening, ready to run like hell. But no one

131

came to investigate. Gingerly he picked out shards of glass and laid them aside, then crawled into the store, wishing for a light.

He was in a workroom or office. His eyes were adjusted to the dark, and he could see two desks, back to back. He opened drawers, struck a match and in the light found a few coins. Putting out the light, he went into the front of the store and groped under the long counter. He could see the street through the front windows and was afraid to light a match. But after a few minutes he came across a small wooden box. He took it into the back and there lit a match. He had eighteen dollars in bills and some coins.

He struck another match and looked through a cabinet. There was a small bottle filled with silver coins, some pipes and a few sacks of Durham. He pocketed the tobacco and bottle and climbed back through the window, annoyed at the small haul. People sure didn't keep much money around . . .

He hurried back to the stable, lighted a candle and counted the coins. Eight dollars and forty-two cents. He dumped them into one of his saddlebags.

Well, it wasn't much, all told, but it would stave off starvation. In the morning he would start by having a good, big breakfast.

★

Chapter 17

Jessica and Ki returned to Gunnison and consulted the map again, to no avail. They asked bartenders—who heard every kind of gossip—and one told them there were copper mines a hundred miles east and south, which was too far away. Besides, the mines were still in operation.

Was there some other place for money to be hidden?

Probably, but one would have to see it—a niche in the rocks, perhaps, a place no one would think of looking.

It was a problem.

Jessie discussed it with Carl Webber and they went riding away from the town. They might have buried the money somewhere, Carl suggested.

"But it would have to be in a place they could easily find again."

"They could have made a map . . ."

Jessie doubted it. "No map was found on Virgil's body —and he would surely have had it—or a copy. He was the leader, after all."

"Maybe he hid the map somewhere."

Jessie laughed. "And made another map to find the first one?"

"The criminal mind is very devious."

"But not necessarily dumb."

Carl laughed. "Not dumb enough to bury maps all over the landscape."

They got down in a clump of trees on the slope of a gentle hill. They could see the rooftops of the town several miles away.

He said, "Mr. Thompson has raised the reward to three thousand dollars."

"He is a headstrong man," Jessie said, shaking her head. "Imagine, offering that much for the return of a million dollars."

They sat on the grass. "What would you do with that much money?"

She smiled. "Probably give most of it away. What would you do with it?"

"I'd buy the territory of Arizona and give it to you."

She leaned close and kissed him fondly. "I don't really need the territory of Arizona."

"That's what you think now . . ." He lowered her to the grass and rubbed her nose with his. "But if you had it . . ."

Her arms went about him.

They only undressed part way, enough to make sensual love in the dappled shade of the surrounding trees.

It was a long time before they lay quiet in each other's arms as the sun started its long plunge to the prairie grass.

When they stirred, Carl leaned on an elbow and looked down at her. "You are the most beautiful thing this side of St Louis . . ."

"Oh? What about the other side?"

"I've never been there. I only speak of what I know."

"You spoke of Arizona . . ."

"Yes, I've been there many times. Where are you going when you leave here?"

"I don't know. But I'm definitely going to find out what happened to Mr. Thompson's gold."

"D'you think Joel Dewey knows?"

"Yes. If he's still alive."

They rode back to town by a roundabout way; Jessie went to the hotel and met Ki in the lobby. He was reading the newspapers from the east.

"Not a word about Dewey. He's dropped from sight."

"I was just talking about him with Carl Webber." She sat by him. "If we could find him . . ."

"That would solve it. Yes." Ki folded the papers. "He could be right here in Gunnison for all we know."

"With Floyd Hicks?"

Ki shrugged. "That's an interesting question."

Floyd Hicks was very annoyed. He went out to the stable and kicked the stall. That damned Joel had been with him for days—days! And never said a damned thing about the robbery or the million dollars!

Of course that meant he had no intention of sharing it. And now where had he gone?

Joel had mentioned going to Texas . . . to Austin, in fact. He'd said he had kinfolk there. Floyd smiled. Joel was not the smartest biscuit in the pan. He had made a very important mistake.

Floyd saddled his horse and headed south, visions of a shower of gold pieces in his head. God almighty! What could a man do with a million dollars! He could have anything he wanted! Anything!

But of course he had to squeeze the location out of Joel. Squeeze him but not kill him. It shouldn't be too difficult.

First things first, however. He had to find Joel.

It was a long weary way to Texas, across the Red and down to Austin. It took two weeks, and he arrived ragged and hungry. He slept in a stable for ten hours and woke in the middle of the night, when nothing was open. Son of a bitch.

In the morning, after a skimpy breakfast, he began asking about the Dewey family that lived in Austin. No one had heard of them. He told a deputy sheriff that Fred Dewey was his uncle, whom he hadn't seen in a coon's age and wanted to talk to before the old man died. The deputy tried to be helpful but knew only one family named Dewey. The man's name was Alonzo.

Having no idea what Joel's father's name was, Floyd went to see this man Alonzo. He took precautions, watching the house for a time, but no Joel. When he went to the door, the man told him there was no one in the family named Joel.

Floyd retreated. There had to be a family in Austin. Joel wasn't devious enough to have—*Had* Joel put one over on him? Jesus Christ! *Had* he? Joel had ridden with Virgil Ropes for a while—maybe he had picked up some tricks.

But Floyd did not give up too easily. He continued looking for the Dewey family—and did not find it. He asked everyone—bartenders, preachers, a half-dozen whores—no one could help. He had to admit it to himself: Joel had put one over on him.

And now where should he look for Joel? The kid had probably dug up the money by now and was on his way to paradise.

Floyd started back north very depressed.

Joel Dewey followed the stage road for perhaps twenty miles, till it turned south. He went on northwest, trying to guide himself by landmarks—which proved to be almost impossible on the open prairie. In another day he knew himself to be lost again.

But it didn't matter. He was moving west, according to

the sun. As long as the sun helped out he would go that way.

He was out of food by the time he reached Langhorn. His horse had thrown a shoe, and he had to walk the last five or six miles leading the limping animal, which did not improve his disposition.

He left the horse at the blacksmith shop, telling the owner to put on a good-enough, and bought food at the general store. He ate it sitting on a box while the blacksmith worked.

Farrington was about fifty miles, mostly north, he was told. He had come too far south. There was a road that went that way, and he took it the next morning.

The land was flatter, the road easier, and he reached Farrington by evening. And now he had to be cautious. The law was certainly still after him, and they probably knew what he looked like.

He camped outside of town, circled it and went on toward Gunnison at first light.

Now he was on the road where Virgil had turned off to the mine. Of course he was going the opposite direction and the land didn't look the same—Where the hell was the turn-off point?

Had Virgil turned off on a definite path or road? He wasn't sure. He walked the horse, looking at the side of the road, stopping now and then to look at it from the opposite angle . . . and it took three days to reach Gunnison.

When the rooflines of the town came into view, he knew he had gone too far. He waited till dark and rode in to an out-of-the-way store to fill a gunnysack with airtights and cheese wrapped in waxed paper. He told the proprietor he was on his way north to visit his folks.

The man, an old-timer with steel-rimmed glasses, said, "Ain't I seen you b'fore?"

137

"I just passin' through," Joel told him. On the way out, he saw the poster tacked to the wall. It was the prison picture of himself with the caption, WANTED FOR MURDER!

He hurried back to the Farrington road. He'd never get used to seeing that.

He hadn't shaved for several days. That was probably what changed him enough so the old man hadn't recognized him. He decided to let the beard grow.

He made a cold camp on the prairie. How many of those damned posters had been distributed, anyway?

A million dollars was a huge amount of money. Even the eastern newspapers picked up the story of the Gunnison Bank robbery and murders. Editors were intrigued by the mystery. What had happened to the money? A million dollars was hidden out there on the prairie.

Newspapers in different cities printed maps showing Gunnison and the road to Farrington. Their artists also circled areas with captions to say this was where the money was hidden. Every newspaper map was different.

A few dozen eager searchers went out, armed with those maps, and picked over areas a hundred miles from the mines.

J. M. Thompson increased the reward to four thousand dollars for information leading to the recovery of the money.

The law was willing to pay one thousand for information leading to the arrest and conviction of Joel Dewey for the murder of Judson Rails. He was also implicated in the murders of four others.

Floyd Hicks was wanted for the murder of Judson Rails. His prison record was well aired in those eastern papers; he was called a desperado, and the newspaper artists had a field day drawing him with two guns smoking . . .

• • •

Floyd felt utterly frustrated. He had no idea in the world where Joel was likely to be. Joel had said he was an orphan and had no home . . . Floyd thought he could be sure of one thing. Joel would go for the hidden money. He knew Joel was broke.

But where was the money?

All he knew about it was what he read in the newspapers, and he was sure they knew very little. They said the money had been lost between two towns, Gunnison and Farrington. But they were a hundred miles apart. Nobody could search that vast an area in one lifetime.

But he had to start somewhere, and he was closer to Farrington, so he pointed for there. But because his photograph was on reward posters he had to be cautious. He circled the town and halted. Nobody knew where the money was, except Joel, so it could be anywhere, even in the town.

The smart thing to do was to look for Joel. Joel had called himself Joe Biggers. Floyd began to go from one boardinghouse to the next, asking for Joe Biggers.

Chapter 18

Joanna Tredwell, living alone since Homer was in Farrington, read the newspapers about the missing money and gold. A million dollars was apparently buried out on the prairie somewhere. At least the papers thought so.

She thought about it constantly. Virgil had been so close, but he hadn't said a thing. Not one damned thing! He had embraced her in bed, often talking about what they would do when they had the money in their hands.

Sometimes, even when he was atop her, moving sinuously into her, he would whisper to her about New Orleans and what times they were going to have. Then, it had all seemed so close . . .

But where the money was hidden was the mystery. The newspapers were sure it was somewhere on the plains, and admitted at the same time that it might be anywhere at all.

Joanna sat in the kitchen with a cup of coffee in front of her and thought about Virgil, how he had come in from the stable nearly every day.

From the *stable*. He had spent a lot of time in the stable. He had cleaned it out and painted it, inside and out. He knew every nook and cranny, probably better than she did, and he'd had time to alter or change it. What if he had hidden the money there?

She felt her heart beating faster all of a sudden. Virge had spent hours and hours there. He could have made a secret compartment, or two or three, where no one would think of looking. She had never once gone out to the stable while he had been painting it. He could have done anything he wanted! Why not?

No one had ever come to inspect it—the marshal had obviously not given it a thought. Neither had anyone from the bank. The stable was not that far from the open prairie. It would have been no trick at all to drive a wagon down the alley and into the stable without her knowing.

She got up and almost ran outside and across the yard to the stable. It was not a large building. It had a steep four-sided roof that came to a sort of point, where a weather vane presided. It had only two stalls. Her horse was in one of them, looking around at her curiously. Her light buggy waited beside the other stall. There were cribs for fodder and shelves for sacks of oats, and a loft that contained odds and ends. The door to the alley was closed and locked.

There was a dusty coal-oil lamp hanging by a nail near the back door. She unhooked it, lifted the glass and struck a match to light the lamp. Then she went up the ladder to the loft. It was crowded with boxes and forgotten things. There was an old round-topped trunk, empty, smelling of mildew, and beside it a chair that lacked a leg. Why had they kept it? The boxes were dusty. She shook them, pushed them, but none contained anything heavy enough to be gold. She looked into each one and found assorted junk.

There was nothing else in the loft—no hidden nooks. She slapped the dust off her hands and went down the ladder. She blew out the lamp and hung it on the nail again. No money up there.

She looked the rest of the stable over carefully, examining each wall separately for alterations or additions, and found none.

But if Virgil had hidden a fortune in the stable, it would certainly be difficult to locate. He'd see to that. Maybe it was buried in the ground.

The stable had a dirt floor, and she took a hoe and prodded the earth. But it was hard-packed; she could find no soft spot.

Standing in the middle of the floor, she gazed around her, looking at everything. There was really no place to hide anything bulky. Homer had told her the money and gold were in stout wooden boxes.

Could it be buried in the garden? She had never seen Virgil working in the garden—but maybe. She went over every inch, prodding with the hoe handle, and found no dirt that seemed recently disturbed. It would have to be a big hole . . .

Reluctantly she concluded that the money was not there. The newspapers were probably right. He had hidden it out on the prairie somewhere.

Damn you, Virgil!

Joel remembered that it was the southern road the wagons had taken from Gunnison, and following it, he came to and stopped at the ambush point. He dismounted and walked over the spot. He had lain right here and fired at the men with Virgil . . . The wagons had come up the road and halted at the first shot.

Then they had piled the boxes into one buckboard and continued on toward Farrington, exulting because they were now rich!

How far had they gone?

He had been excited and jittery at the time and had paid scant attention, thinking golden thoughts of wine, women and exotic places. Had they gone ten miles or twenty before they turned off? He recalled it as a long time. But he had been anxious to get his hands on the greenbacks.

There was no road that turned off to the right. He was positive it was to the right—west.

He came to a two-track road that wound off to the left, but that could not be the one—could it? Maybe he'd been mixed up that day. He followed the road east for an hour or more till it petered out in a grassy flat.

Swearing, he turned back.

Back on the road, he debated with himself. The mine had been in some low hills. He could see no hills from where he was, but of course, he recalled the mine being a long long way from the road.

He made up his mind and turned the horse's head west, moving across the plain. He halted at dusk to make a deep Indian fire to boil coffee and heat beans in a can.

He had left too damn much to Virgil. He should have been more alert—and this was a fine time to discover it. He had a terrible feeling that he was miles in the wrong direction. The prairie was a vast sea of grass that was swallowing him up. One direction was as good as another. But he could depend on the sun; it always rose in the east.

Except when it clouded over. As he slept, a thick bank of gray clouds came streaming from the west, and he woke in the morning with a clammy mist hanging just over his head.

He slipped into his slicker and made another fire for breakfast. He had not oriented himself the day before; he should have made a mark on the ground to show him how he had been traveling. When he started out he headed south instead of west.

And he did not see the sun for another two days. During that time it rained spasmodically, not enough to make the washes impassable, but enough to make him miserable and cold.

He did not come to any hills at all. But he finally found an overhang along a riverbank, and he hurried into it. He unsaddled the horse and gathered driftwood and branches to make a fire. Being rich wasn't all it was said to be.

He stayed in the niche another day and a half, until the storm grumpily moved east. Then he saddled up again, looked at the weak, watery sun and decided he was far enough west. He rode eastward for three days but saw no hills. Where the hell was the mine?

When he came to the road, he halted. It wandered sort of north and south, curving around small slopes and rises, not a very particular road . . .

Sighing, he followed it north.

And came to Farrington. He sat the horse and stared at the rooftops. He had made a great circle and come back to the same road again, south of the town.

He felt put upon. Not the chosen of God.

He rented a room in a boardinghouse on the outskirts and fell into the bunk bed, exhausted. He remained in the house for two days; it rained on and off . . . winter was coming. It did not help his black mood. Where in hell was the damn mine?

He lay on the bunk bed, staring at the ceiling, trying to remember every detail of that fateful day: how they had torn open the boxes and selected the ones with the gold and money, and ridden away leaving the bodies sprawled in the road. He was positive he would know the mine when he saw it again—if he could only find it.

When the weather cleared he bought victuals and tied them on behind the cantle and rode north, following the road to Gunnison. He had to try it again.

It was a moody day when he sat set out; a cold wind blew across the plains, flinging bits of dirt and grass. A few grouse jumped into the air and beat away frantically when he came close. He plodded on, following the road and studying each inch of the western side of it. Where the hell had they turned off?

He remembered that Virgil had gone back and swept away all evidence of their passing. That was what was keeping him from finding the turnoff. He sat the horse and sighed deeply. Cloud shadows crossed the long prairie swells, and the land seemed to move and stir . . . For the first time he began to realize that he might never find the mine again!

In late afternoon he saw the other rider.

A man on a gray horse appeared on a rise, perhaps a mile away, too far to recognize him—but Joel had a feeling the man was Floyd.

And if he were, Floyd was seeking him.

Joel turned his horse instantly and rode out of sight. Had the other man seen him? If Floyd were coming after him, it meant that Floyd knew about the money and wanted it.

He spurred away to the south, avoiding high ground, wishing for dark.

Floyd had seen him. He had seen a rider who turned away instantly on seeing another human—not a likely thing under ordinary circumstances. Two pilgrims meeting far out in the sticks were eager to trade news or talk, as a rule. Unless one happened to be on the outs with the law.

Or, in Joel's case, unwilling to share in a fortune.

He followed south, keeping to high ground when he could, to see farther. He had several glimpses of the other rider but could not close with him.

He swore terrible oaths when dusk came, knowing he would lose the rider . . . and he did.

Finally he halted where he'd last seen him and made camp. Maybe he could track him in the morning . . .

★

Chapter 19

Jessica said, "I've got an itchy feeling about something . . ."

"What?"

"Sheriff Ben Elsby."

Ki was surprised. "What do you mean, an itchy feeling?"

"I don't know. But what if he didn't tell us all he knew?"

"Why would he hold out?"

"The reward. It's three thousand now, isn't it?"

"Four thousand."

"That's a lot of money."

Ki nodded. "How long have you had this itchy feeling?"

"A few weeks. But I felt rather silly about it—it's only a hunch of course . . . probably sheer foolishness."

Ki mused. "Underhill *is* the last place Virgil was seen alive . . ."

"But it's a long trip."

He studied her. "You don't have very many hunches. Is this a good strong one?"

She smiled. "Well . . . I suppose so. Do we have

a better lead in another direction?"

"No. Unless we can find Joel Dewey, I'm afraid the case is closed . . . the money is lost."

"Then it wouldn't hurt anything for us to go talk to Elsby."

"Nothing at all."

Joel spurred his horse south and, when it was full dark, turned east. The mine was somewhere west, but Floyd didn't know that. No one knew it but himself.

He rode most of the night, walking the horse, putting miles between him and his pursuer. He would make another great circle and come out west of Farrington. Floyd would wander about and finally give up. What else could he do?

In early morning Joel came to some hills that rose straight out of the flat land and, as he worked through them, came to a deep gully. It had a sandy bottom, and he followed it for several miles, then selected a niche and got down to roll in his blanket for a badly needed sleep.

He woke in very late afternoon, feeling refreshed. It was only a short while till dusk. He decided to stay where he was for the night. Floyd could not possibly be anywhere near.

In the morning, when he broke camp and rode on, Joel discovered another camper only about a mile away. The man looked like a prospector. He had a gray, straggly beard and weather-beaten clothes, and a mule. He was surprised to see Joel.

"Thought ever'body had give up and gone back to town."

"Give up on what?" Joel asked.

"The bank money, a course. Ain't that what you lookin' for?"

Joel made a face. Somewhere he had read that people were out looking for the gold. Here was one of them. He

148

said, "First I heard of it." He pretended great surprise.

"Hell's fire, half the territory's out lookin' for it."

"I ain't seen nobody," Joel said.

"Where you come from?"

"Over west."

"Well, that's why then." The other said, "My name's Jacks. What's yourn?"

"Smith."

"Well, they ain't no gold hid over west, Mr. Smith. It's here some'eres."

"It's hid?"

"You bet. It's in a hole'r something. I been a-lookin' the last two months."

Joel was fascinated to hear what the other man had to say. "How you know it's around here?"

"Newspapers say so. I got 'em in m'kick there."

"The money's hid in a hole?"

"Got to be," Jacks said. "I notice you ain't got a shovel. So you didn't know about it, huh?"

"No, I sure didn't." It occurred to Joel for the first time that he would have to have a shovel to dig into the mine. The one they had was burned up in the wagon fire.

Jacks was talking. Joel said, "What?"

"You must be driftin' through."

Joel nodded. "That's right." Damn, he would have to go to Farrington and buy a shovel. Or maybe he could steal one . . . and a pick. What the hell good would it do him to find the mine and then not be able to dig out the money . . . ?

Jacks was saying, "Where you headed?"

"Huh? Oh . . . just south . . . guess I'll go down Texas way . . ." Son of a bitch. Why hadn't he thought of that before? Now he'd have to head west and find the Gunnison road again.

He said good-bye to the prospector, who stared at him, and rode off.

Jacks said aloud, looking after him. "He ain't right in the goddam head."

It was a long ride to Underhill, and it rained once, driving them under some trees to wait it out. There was no lightning with the storm, and when the rain let up they went on, holding the slickers tightly around them against the cold. And when they halted for the night, Ki built two warming fires and they sat between them.

Underhill was on the flats, near a large spring-fed pond; possibly the start of the town was there. The houses and other buildings spread west in the center of the lush valley. Jessie and Ki entered the main street; it was very wide, crowded in places with wagons and horsemen. There was a large open-air market and off it the sheriff's office.

They got down and went inside. A slim young deputy nodded to them from behind a desk, then took a second look at Jessica.

"What can I do for you folks?" He got up quickly as she smiled.

She said, "We'd like to speak to Sheriff Elsby."

"So would we, ma'am."

"What?"

The deputy looked from one to the other, "We ain't seen him for a while. He up and disappeared."

Ki said, "Disappeared? A sheriff has disappeared?"

"That's right. Nobody knows where he went. Wife, us, nobody."

"He said nothing to anyone?"

"Not that we can find out, ma'am. His wife is as surprised as anybody else. He left one day just like always and never came back. Left no note or nothing."

Jessie looked at Ki. "All right," she smiled at the deputy, "thank you." They went out to the street.

Ki said, "Is it connected to the bank robbery?"

"It could be anything of course—an old enemy who bushwhacked him and buried the body . . ."

"Do you think so?"

"No. Do you?"

Ki shrugged. "Coincidences bother mè."

"And the fact of a million dollars hidden somewhere on the prairie."

He smiled. "That bothers me more. So we both suspect that Elsby found a clue to it?"

"That he didn't tell us about. Yes."

"Then it pretty much had to be something he found on Virgil's body."

Jessica nodded. "I'd guess so." She shook her head. "Damn him. We could probably have finished this a long time ago . . ."

"A million does things to people. What's our next move? There's nothing for us here."

"Back to Gunnison?"

He nodded.

Ben Elsby thought about the letter for days. Virgil Ropes had written a short letter to someone in New Orleans but had not posted it, possibly because he'd not had a chance to do it without his companions knowing.

The letter said that he, Virgil, had come into money and had hidden it in a mine shaft. He would go back for it and come to New Orleans, and they would celebrate together. The letter was addressed to Marie Santos and asked her to say nothing to anyone about him. He expected to see her soon.

Ben spent a few days telegraphing for information—he

151

was the sheriff, after all. He learned that the robber-killers had ambushed the wagons at a particular spot and had disappeared. Virgil and the other man had then hidden the money and were obviously waiting for the hue and cry to diminish.

So, if he, Ben Elsby, went to the ambush point and started his search from there, looking for a mine shaft, he was bound to find it sooner or later. That was logic, wasn't it? And when he found it he'd be rich. He would leave Underhill behind and go east and enjoy the rest of his days spending the money.

He had heard that particular story from outlaws many times before in his years as a lawman. But he had never thought he would be saying it himself.

He spent several hours arranging his disappearance. He bought food, took clothes and weapons to a hiding place, and then one morning kissed his wife and rode away, saying only that he was making rounds.

He went straight across the plains and hills toward Gunnison.

Chapter 20

Floyd Hicks found tracks and followed them eastward, sure that he was on Joel's trail. But he was not the best tracker and lost them half a dozen times. The tracks led generally east, however, so he was able to pick them up if he circled ahead. It was slow going.

And he lost the tracks finally in the rain.

Was Joel heading for the cache? Probably. What else would he be doing out here in the middle of nowhere?

The thought occurred to Floyd, when he made camp, that Joel had seen him and led him on a long wild goose chase. Maybe Joel wasn't heading for the treasure but was merely trying to throw him off the track. That was very possible. And even if Joel was dumb as hell, he still might be capable of it.

When he got up the next morning and looked around at the rolling land, Floyd decided he would never find one man in all that vastness. He would go back to the road and wait. If Joel was making a false trail, he might come back to the starting point. He might. Floyd didn't have a better idea.

Jessica and Ki returned to Gunnison and made inquiries about Ben Elsby. Had anyone seen him? Only a few had heard his name; no one had seen him.

Ki thought it unlikely that Virgil had made a map showing the exact location of the cache. "He wouldn't know whose hands it might fall into."

Jessie tended to agree. "But Elsby must know something we don't . . ."

"Maybe he thinks he knows something."

She said, "You're talking in riddles. He either knows something or he doesn't."

"Maybe he's doing some guesswork."

She laughed. "We do that all the time. Let's guess where he is."

"I'd say he went first to the ambush point. That's where it all started. Our problem is we don't know in which direction Virgil and Joel went from there. They had 360 degrees to choose from."

"Are you saying that maybe Elsby knows which direction?"

Ki grinned. "Maybe. That would give him some kind of edge, wouldn't it?"

"Yes, it would."

Jessica went to call on Joanna Tredwell. It was possible the woman had forgotten something.

But she maintained that she had not. "I know nothing at all about the robbery. Homer told me nothing. As you certainly know by now, it was a big secret kept by Harrison Edwards and JM."

"But how did Virgil know where to meet the wagons that day?"

"I have no idea. Probably he kept a watch on the bank and followed them."

"Were you able to narrow the date down for him?"

Joanna rose regally. "I have nothing further to say to you, Miss Starbuck. Please have the goodness to leave."

There was nothing to do but comply. Jessie told Ki, "I'm sure she had some information from Tredwell."

"And she'll never admit it for fear of complicity."

"Exactly."

A telegram came for them from J. M. Thompson, asking them to come to Farrington.

"He's unhappy," Ki predicted. "He'll ask us questions that have no answers . . ."

Carl Webber was not pleased to see them go. He rode several miles down the Farrington trail with Jessie, asking her to promise she would return.

She kissed him fondly. "I will if it's possible."

"I think you can make almost anything possible . . ."

"I wish I had your confidence."

They found Thompson in his office in the Farrington Bank. He was the same stout, fish-eyed, florid man, dressed in a black frock coat and silk necktie. He asked them to enter and pointed to chairs.

"What have you learned?"

Jessie said, "We think your money is still safely hidden, Mr. Thompson."

"That's a supposition."

"Yes, of course. I wish we had the money to give you."

Thompson took a turn up and down the turkey carpet. "If we go along this way, I will not have the money ten years from now." His face became a shade darker. "I have written a letter to the Comstock Detective Agency in Kansas City, asking them to send an agent or two. I am determined to get to the bottom of this, and I do not believe you two are doing it."

Jessie rose at once. She smiled at Thompson, looked at Ki and went to the door without a word. Ki hurried to open the door for her. He nodded to JM, closed the door, and they walked downstairs to the street.

"I knew he'd be unhappy," Ki said.

"I doubt if he's ever been anything but." She faced Ki. "Now we have a decision. Do we stay or go?"

Ki shrugged. "I hate to give up in the middle of a job."

"So do I."

"I think we ought to go looking for Joel Dewey."

Jessie smiled. "Agreed."

Ben Elsby was not the slim, muscled young man he once had been. He had grown comfortably stout about the middle and was unused to camping out in the wilds. He had keen young deputies for that kind of work.

But his deputies were in Underhill and he was on his own—but not for long. He had drawn a good wad of money from the bank before he left town, and it made a comforting weight in his saddlebags.

It was a long ride from Underhill. He managed to miss the rain but was exhausted by the time he reached Farrington. He rented a hotel room, giving his name as Ben Ellsworth. He rested for two days, then took the Gunnison road north. He had a detailed description of the ambush point in his pocket and easily located it.

From there he rode east for several miles, looking for a mine shaft. He was sure the killers had gone east because that was the quickest way out of the territory—as several newspaper stories had mentioned. In his experience, thieves and killers liked to get as far from the crime as possible as soon as possible.

The hiding place, he was sure, could not be far. The gold was too heavy to carry across country too far—the wagon was likely to break down. And the killers had only a buckboard. They must have disposed of it. All the police reports that had come across his desk were positive on one point. No strangers with wagons had gone through any town on those dates, or near them, within a hundred-mile radius. All stage-line and railroad depots had been carefully checked. The police were good at those tasks. Elsby was sure the information could be depended upon.

So the treasure was buried in the mine shaft, waiting for the killers to return.

He put himself in the killers' place. They would drive the wagon from where they had ambushed the guards and drivers, but not too far. Some wandering pilgrim might see them and remember.

In about five miles' distance, Elsby began to look for the mine shaft. Virgil's letter had not been explicit. It had said only "mine shaft." Very vague. Of course Virgil was writing to a woman who probably wouldn't know a mine shaft from a goat.

A mine shaft could be anything—a hole in the ground or an elaborate wood-shored tunnel. He doubted it would be the latter.

He found nothing that might be it.

He rode over and around, back and forth and still found nothing that could be a mine.

And it began to rain.

Swearing a blue streak, he headed back to Farrington. He rented the same room again and waited out the storm.

When it had passed, he hired a buckboard, bought a tent, a shovel and sacks of food and set out again, determined this time to stay longer, to make a better search.

He returned to the ambush point and moved east as before. This time he went about ten miles before pulling up to make camp. He would leave the wagon here and ride the surrounding country, then move the wagon and ride the country again, methodically.

Sooner or later he would stumble on it. A million dollars was a lot of incentive.

But a week later he had still found nothing.

Joel Dewey rode into Farrington very slowly after dark. It was closer than Gunnison, but he might be known to the local law—if they happened to see him.

He needed a mule and some tools and, after counting his money, decided he would have to steal them. It was easy to locate a tethered mule, but he had to enter a barn or toolshed to find tools. He tried several barns and stables and was driven off each time by dogs—until he found one without a canine guard.

It was very late, so he took a chance, and struck a match and quickly put his hands on a pick and shovel and a sturdy pack tree. He toted them all to the outskirts and went back for the mule. He had seen one in a nearby corral.

He lifted off the poles and led the mule out, put the poles back and in another hour was on the Gunnison road again.

This time he would find the mine.

★

Chapter 21

Winter had other plans for all of them. It rained for three days, then the rain turned to snow. Jessica and Ki retreated to the hotel in Farrington, confident that Joel Dewey was holed up out of the elements, and not out on the open prairie with a shovel.

Joel was in fact twenty miles from Farrington, heading north when the storm swept over the land. He gave way before it and let it push him south into the little town of Kimber. He bypassed Farrington with his stolen mule and got a room in the only hotel, seventy-five cents a day.

The room was cold, but there was a belly stove downstairs with a footring. He could afford to stay only a short while—unless he could acquire more money somewhere. He walked through the town, looking at prospects. They did not seem favorable. And anyway, it made him nervous to think of robbing someone in the town and then staying there.

Why not wait for a break in the storm and ride to Farrington? There would be better chances there.

There was a wanted poster with his picture on it in the hotel lobby. However, Joel had not shaved for two weeks; his beard was straggly, but at least he looked nothing like the photo.

In a week the storm passed, and a faint sun came out in a cold sky, and Joel counted his money again. He had enough to stay a few more days.

That afternoon he started for Farrington.

He arrived the next day and rode through the town streets like any drifter, looked at stores and back alleys and selected a general store as the best prospect. It had a door on an alley, no window on the ground floor but several higher up. Joel thought he could climb in one.

He whiled away the hours in a saloon, then rode around to the alley after full dark. He tied the horse and waited long minutes, listening and watching. He approached the back of the store and tried the door, but it was locked, so he began to climb to the nearest window.

A voice spoke out of nowhere: "Get down from there!"

Joel turned to look in astonishment. A man stood by the door with a pistol pointed at his middle. Where the hell had he come from?

"Get down!"

Joel climbed down, then saw the glint of the star on the man's chest. He put his hands up and the man took his revolver. The man motioned. "Start walking."

"You a sheriff?"

"Deputy Town Marshal."

"I wasn't meaning no harm . . ."

" 'Course not." The marshal chuckled. "You was just a-climbin' up there for fun. You do that all the time, do you?"

He put Joel in a jail cell and slammed the door.

The next day he was brought in front of a judge, a thin, embittered-looking man who regarded Joel as if he might be a bug on a pin. "This the defendant?"

"He's the one goin' to rob McKlain's store, Your Honor."

The judge stared at Joel. "You been up before me in the past?"

"No sir," Joel said.

"You got any money?"

Joel shook his head. "I'm down on m'luck, sir."

"Marshal, you seen him going in the store?"

"He was climbin' in the back way, Your Honor, going to break in a window."

"Did he break the window?"

"No, but—"

The judge rapped with his gavel. "Three months." He motioned. "What's next?"

The marshal took Joel by the arm and led him out and into the jail. The cell door slammed behind him again.

The Comstock Detective Agency sent one of its agents, Philip Bone, to Farrington to see Mr. J. M. Thompson.

Bone was a lean, brown-faced man in a store suit and a bowler hat. He took a room at the main hotel and sent a boy to the bank with a note to say he had arrived and to ask for an appointment.

Thompson sent the boy back to say Bone should come at once.

Thompson received him with Harrison Edwards; they shook hands and Bone sat to listen. Both JM and Edwards filled him in on the robbery and murders. It took an hour.

What Thompson wanted was the recovery of the money, amounting to about a million dollars in cash and gold.

Bone whistled at the amount. "So this Virgil Ropes is dead, and now the only one who knows where the money is is Joel Dewey?"

"That's the way it looks," Edwards said. "Unless he's told someone else."

JM had one of the posters. "This is what he looks like."

Bone studied it. "He's young?"

"About twenty I'd guess," Edwards replied.

161

"How about friends, relatives, home . . . ?"

JM shook his head. "He's an orphan, so far as we know. He rode with a man named Floyd Hicks for a short time. We don't know where Hicks is now."

Bone said, "Floyd Hicks was in jail a short time ago."

"Yes, but he's out now."

"Could he and Joel Dewey be together?"

Edwards shrugged. "Certainly, they could be, yes. We don't know."

Bone said, "So you moved everything the bank owned from Gunnison to here, but the only time you moved the money it was robbed?"

"That's right."

"Then it was someone in your employ who informed, Mr. Thompson. Someone here is guilty."

JM nodded. "We thought so, too. But who?"

"Everyone in the bank was double-checked, Mr. Bone," Edwards said quickly. "We think the killers heard about the move and watched the bank."

"All right, but how did they know which delivery to hit?"

"We don't know. No one knew which one it was but me."

JM said, " *I* didn't even know."

Bone studied Edwards. "I see." He got up. "Then I should start looking for young Joel Dewey." He looked at the poster again, folded it and put it in his pocket.

Ben Elsby sat in his tent for several days while it rained. He smoked cigars and slept. A man his age should be sitting by his fire at home . . . But a million dollars was worth some hardship . . .

He would stick it out, no matter what. And he tried. He stayed through a terrible storm, but finally the weather drove him back to Farrington. There was no possibility he could find the mine shaft under those conditions.

He took to sitting in the Bird Cage Saloon, sipping beer and playing solitaire to pass the hours.

Every now and then someone came in discussing the robbery and the missing million dollars. Elsby listened attentively to the various theories. One thought the money had long ago been taken east or west to San Francisco. Another was sure it was lost forever. Someone else was positive it was here in Farrington . . .

It was amusing. He, Benjamin Elsby, was the only person who really knew where it was.

In a manner of speaking.

Floyd Hicks camped out near the Gunnison road for a week or more, hoping that Joel would show up. He never did. When it began to rain in earnest, and snow a little, he hurried to the nearest town, Gunnison, and took a room in a cheap boarding house, giving his name as Fred Hanks.

He spent the next week dodging in and out of saloons, looking for Joel. The man had to be somewhere . . . He sipped beer and listened to conversations, hoping to hear a word that would lead him to Joel. Talk of the million dollars lying out on the prairie was dying out. People had talked of it so much there was nothing further to say. They began to get back to the normal topics: money and women.

After a week, Floyd was sure Joel was not in this town. However, he made the rounds of boarding and rooming houses, asking for him, and turned up nothing.

He decided to go to Farrington, between rainstorms.

But winter set in fast and hard, and the day he had planned to leave dawned icy cold and snowing.

He stayed where he was.

• • •

Spring came early, ushering in warmer days and green grass. Floyd packed his warbag and rode out toward Farrington, glad to be moving.

The road was muddy; there were puddles everywhere, but the air was fresh and clean, and he had a feeling he would find Joel and the money soon. He felt lucky.

Halfway to Farrington he made camp by the road before dark, and as he built a fire a stranger appeared. He was a lean man, deeply tanned, and wore nearly new jeans and a heavy brown coat. A Colt revolver was handy to his right hand. He halted and waited politely for a word to get down.

Floyd said, "I got coffee a-makin'. Light and set."

"Thanks." The man got down and found a dry spot. "I'm heading for Gunnison. Name's Philip Bone."

"Fred Hanks," Floyd said, pushing sticks into the fire. He shook the coffee pot and got out another tin cup.

As he poured the other man said, "I'm looking for a man named Floyd Hicks. You happen to know him?"

Floyd's hand shook and he set the cup down quickly, "Damn, too hot." He shook his head. "Don't know 'im. What's he done? You a lawman?"

"Private detective. Hicks is wanted in connection with the Gunnison Bank robbery. I guess you heard of it."

"Ever'body heard of that one." They sipped the coffee. Floyd stared at the detective. He had seldom been so close to a lawman without the other putting shackles on him. Bone looked like any cowboy, maybe a little more prosperous.

Bone asked, "You come from Gunnison?"

"Yes . . ."

"How far is it?"

"Maybe five hours."

Bone looked at the sky. "Think I'll go on then. Got

a feeling I'll find Hicks there." He got up. "Thanks for the coffee . . ." He mounted the horse, waved and went past.

Floyd looked after the man. Five hours to Gunnison! It was more like a full day. He was unable to tell the truth to a lawman. To hell with them. It was a familiar feeling, being wanted by the law. But he was glad of the warning; how many other lawmen were in the area, looking for him?

In the morning he was up early and on the road. He met no one else till he got close to Farrington, then there were a few riders and a woman driving a buckboard.

He got a room, put his horse in the stable and went out to look for Joel. Million dollar Joel, the little son of a bitch! Why hadn't he said he knew about the loot? Jesus! You couldn't trust anyone anymore.

There was too much land; he would never explore it all. He could cover maybe thirty miles in a day, looking for niches or holes or caves . . . He would grow old looking for the damned money. Or for Joel Dewey.

Floyd sighed, staring around him. It was impossible, the needle in the haystack. One man could not do it.

But two men would double the odds.

What if he returned to Farrington and wired Lucas Pitt? He and Lucas had ridden together and had had some high old times before he'd gone to jail. Maybe Lucas would be interested in half a million dollars.

It was easy to give away half of something he didn't have.

In Farrington he wired Lucas Pitt a carefully composed message. In two hours he had a reply. Lucas was interested but wanted more details. After all, it was a long trip from Kansas to Farrington.

Floyd wrote Lucas a detailed letter and posted it that night.

Philip Bone looked over the ambush point. The bushwhackers had piled the money and gold into one wagon—one wagon had been missing—and driven off with it.

Most likely they had gone along the road, one way or the other. Why shouldn't they? Who was to stop them? It would be the quickest way to leave the scene. Then they could cut across the prairie . . . anywhere they chose.

The wagon had never been found either.

He lit a cigar and puffed smoke. What would *he* have done? Of course that depended on what the thieves had planned. *He* would have had a hiding place in mind and would have gone to it . . . if he had decided to hide the money.

If he had not hidden the money, then what? He would have transported it out of the area, probably to the far east. How would he have done that?

He consulted the map J. M. Thompson had given him. There were two railroad possibilities. But in order to put the loot on a railroad baggage car he would have had to recrate it, make it look like something else. The law watched every stage-line and railroad depot.

But even if he had recrated it, the law might very well have ordered the box opened. He was certain that would have happened. There was too much at stake.

So the railroad was out. And the stage, too. The gold and money would make too big a package for a stagecoach. Had someone made up a dozen small boxes and shipped them that way? But wouldn't that be suspicious?

He frowned at the end of the cigar. It was looking more and more as if they had hidden the loot, to come back for it later.

And that theory tied in with the known facts. Virgil Ropes had been killed in a robbery attempt. That proved he needed money—when he had a million of the bank's assets. Why did he need money? Because the loot was hidden.

It all came back to that.

It was guesswork, which way they had gone. Philip Bone hated to rely on guesses. He was a man of facts. Facts led to success in detective work. He finished the cigar and tossed it away.

Then he returned to Farrington and went to the marshal's office. Had anyone stumbled across the wagon that had been used to haul away the loot?

No one had. The marshal was out, and a deputy had just brought a prisoner's meal from the nearby restaurant. There was only one prisoner in the jail, a ragged, scraggly-bearded man who cowered away from him. Bone shook his head at the creature and waited in the office while the deputy shoved the tray under the bars.

They had moved heaven and hell looking for the wagon, the deputy told him. "But it didn't turn up nowhere. We figger they must have burned it up."

Bone sighed. That was likely. "What about Joel Dewey? Did he have any known haunts?"

"Not that we know of. He's only about twenty."

"He's got to be somewhere!"

The deputy shrugged. "He could be in Baltimore for all we know. If I was him, I might be."

Bone grunted. He went back to the hotel frustrated. The case ended at the ambush point. A dead end. There were no leads at all in any direction.

Over supper in the dining room, he decided to talk to Homer Tredwell. Tredwell had been questioned and requestioned, he knew . . . but there was always a chance. In his opinion, Tredwell and his wife were closest to

Virgil Ropes and might be in collusion. If indeed they knew where the money was, they would probably act exactly as they were acting—pretending to be estranged—until it was safe to dig up the loot.

Tredwell was easy to find but hard to talk to. At first he refused to talk to a private detective. "I don't have to say a word to you."

"If you're not guilty of anything . . . why are you worried?"

"I said nothing about being worried."

"Did you know Virgil Ropes at all, Mr. Tredwell?"

"No."

"But you paid him to paint your stable."

"My wife paid him. I never saw the man."

"You never met him, never saw him at all?"

"Never."

"How did he happen to come to your house to paint the stable?"

Tredwell shrugged. "I don't know."

"Did your wife know him?"

Tredwell was annoyed. "Why don't you go ask her?"

"What about Joel Dewey? Did you know him?"

"No."

"You never met him?"

"No. Never."

"Do you bear a grudge against J. M. Thompson?"

Tredwell sniffed. "If I did, I wouldn't tell you."

"I see."

"I have work to do Mr. . . . whatever your name is." Homer pointed to the door.

Bone left, having learned nothing, but with suspicions alive. Tredwell could be lying to him. There was something there . . . he could not put his finger on it . . .

• • •

168

Jessica said, "Everyone tells us that Joel Dewey is not smart. But he has eluded everyone, so far as we know. He must have a secret hideout."

"Or he's dead. Why isn't it possible that Floyd Hicks has found him, squeezed information out of him and buried him somewhere?"

She sighed. "Yes, that's possible." She smiled ruefully. "I don't like it much, but it's possible. It's also possible that Sheriff Elsby has found Joel."

Ki made a face. "I think that's farfetched."

"We shouldn't overlook anything."

"Well, it'll soon be summer again. It's been months since the robbery-murders, and the chances of Joel or someone else getting the money onto a railroad baggage car are improving."

They were in Gunnison, and Jessica talked that evening with Carl Webber. He had a flyer from Thompson at the Farrington Bank. "He's recruiting men for a posse."

"Thompson is?"

"Yes." He showed her the paper. "He wants fifty or a hundred men to comb the prairies looking for Joel Dewey. He's offering good day wages . . ."

"I'll be darned." Jessie chuckled. "Will it turn up Joel, or just drive him away? Isn't Joel going to read one of these flyers, too?"

"Possibly. I'd say that Thompson is getting panicky about his money. He fears he'll never see any of it again."

She nodded. "It'll be interesting to see who it turns up."

"Probably some jackrabbits and a few rattlesnakes, maybe a prospector or two . . . but not Joel. It would be too easy to evade a hundred men. He'd see them coming a mile away."

"I'm afraid you're right."

"But Thompson will do as he pleases. I guess he can

hire anyone he wants." Carl smiled. "I wonder how long he'll keep it up." He ran his finger along her arm. "I'm officially off duty in ten minutes . . ."

"And I'll officially be in room six." She rose, grinning down at him. "Shall I expect you?"

It was not only confining in the jail, but it was usually cold. The local law did not provide a stove for prisoners, so Joel often stayed in bed, wrapped in his blankets, shivering.

They had taken his knife from him also, so his beard and hair had grown longer and longer till he resembled a hermit from the far hills.

He had given his name as John Biggs from Omaha, which no one had questioned. He was small fry after all.

But he had his dreams. He lay on the bunk and dreamed of his riches. He spent hours in fantastic details, the coffeehouses of New Orleans, which Virgil had told him about, the bordellos, the gambling houses . . .

The months dragged by.

Outside the jail people were looking for him everywhere.

Ben Elsby was the only one looking for a mine shaft. His only hope was that he would find it before Joel returned to it. As soon as the weather showed signs of spring, he was out again with his buckboard, combing the prairie.

He had evolved a new system. Starting at the ambush point, he made concentric circles around that spot, moving out wider and wider, like ripples in a pond, examining every inch of ground.

It was thorough, but extremely time-consuming—and several times while making laps he became confused and wandered off, finding himself miles away when he reached the road again. But that was to be expected on the lonesome plains.

★

Chapter 22

Lucas Pitt read Floyd's letter with mounting interest. Floyd offered him one half of a million dollars—if they could find it. The loot was hidden somewhere on the prairie not far from Gunnison, Floyd thought.

Two could cover more ground than one.

But there was a time element. One person knew where the treasure was hidden, Floyd wrote, and they would have to find it before that person returned to it.

It added spice to the hunt . . . or did it?

But whatever, the huge amount of loot was worth the trip. Lucas got his traps together, stole a horse and saddle and hit the trail. He had invested time in jobs before that had promised scant return. This one would fix him for life, as Floyd said.

He sent Floyd a wire saying he would come to Farrington, which was closer. They would meet there and begin the search together.

He dreamed about the riches during the long trip.

But when he arrived he saw that Floyd was not in the same elated mood. Floyd had no idea where the loot was buried, not even an idea of the area to be searched. Somehow Lucas had expected a short search and much booty.

He was annoyed that Floyd had not told him the exact truth.

Floyd said, "I told you we'd have to hunt for it."

"I thought you meant in a square mile or something, not the whole goddam prairie from here to the Rocky Mountains!"

"It's not that bad . . ."

"You tell me about this road from here to Gunnison. You don't even know which side of the road to look!"

"It's prob'ly on the east side."

"Prob'ly . . ." Lucas shook his head. "Floyd, you don't know your ass!"

Floyd's tone was sullen. "Well, I know it's a million dollars."

"And where is this Joel Dewey?"

"I don't know."

Lucas blew out his breath. "By now he's prob'ly gone and dug it up and is somewheres spending it. Ain't that possible?"

Floyd shrugged. "Are you gonna help search or not?"

"I think you got as much chance of findin' it as I have of gettin' hen eggs from a duck."

"Does that mean no?"

"That means *no*." Lucas stalked out, got on his horse and headed east.

Jessica and Ki could find no trace of Joel Dewey. It was as if the man had dropped into a well. No one had seen him, there was no evidence of his passing, no matter where they looked.

Ki said, "I think he dug up some of the money and is spending it in London . . . or Paris."

Jessie laughed . . . then sobered. "What am I laughing at? He could be."

They traveled the prairie at random, hoping to catch sight of him, and did not.

But while they were moving east of the Gunnison road, Jessie halted suddenly. "I just saw a glint of metal." She pointed and Ki got out his binoculars. He focused them and swept the terrain slowly, then stopped.

"It's a man with a buckboard. He looks familiar . . ." He handed her the glasses.

She took a long look. "It's Ben Elsby." She passed the binocs back, and Ki confirmed it.

"You're right! So that's what's become of him. He's a treasure hunter!"

"And he must have good reason to be out here . . . He must have found something on Virgil's body."

"Shall we talk to him?"

Jessie frowned. "He won't tell us anything, will he?"

"I doubt it."

"Then why don't we just watch him. If he knows where the money is, we'll let him dig it up, then move in."

"Good enough."

Philip Bone called on Joanna Tredwell in Gunnison. She was the one who had entertained Virgil Ropes. She was the obvious link, and he was positive the other investigators had overlooked something. She had to know more than she had told.

It was even possible, since Virgil's partner, Joel Dewey, could not be found, that she was hiding him. She had to be part of the plot.

He watched the house for several days and nights, hoping to see Joel. But no one but Joanna went in or out.

He rapped on her door, and she was hardly civil when he told her he had questions for her.

"Leave me alone." She closed the door in his face.

He rapped again, and she shouted through the door that she would call for the marshal.

He got nowhere at all.

He talked to Marshal Jack Coleman and discovered that Coleman had had her in jail but was now convinced that Virgil had duped her, that she knew nothing about where the money was hidden.

He said, "I searched her house when she was out. It's not there. It's not anywhere on her property."

"But she has to be the link—"

"I thought so, too. But she isn't."

"Then why did Virgil Ropes hang around her? It had to be because her husband was a bank officer. Virgil got information through her."

Coleman nodded. "We all thought that, Mr. Bone. But if he did, we can't prove a thing. Both Joanna and her husband swear he told her nothing."

Philip Bone sat in a saloon and had several drinks, reflecting that he was at a dead end. The case could not be solved without Joel Dewey . . . and he could not be found.

There was only one thing to do, return to Farrington and report to J. M. Thompson that the case was closed. Joel was probably dead. It had been several months since anyone had heard from him.

Ben Elsby gave up making circles. He drifted from one place to another, looking for a mine shaft. It could be anywhere. He knew nothing at all about mining or prospecting. He supposed there were favorable locations for ore, and maybe he would be smart to hire someone who knew such things . . .

But if he hired someone and then found the treasure, that someone would want half or at least a share. It would only mean trouble in the end.

As he sat one night by a tiny warming fire, he considered. He had spent most of his time east of the Gunnison road, thinking it the most likely direction. But it might be west of the road. It *might* be.

In the morning he packed up and headed west. He crossed the road and continued for two days, wandering here and there, but nothing looked like a possibility, until he stood on a rise and noticed the blur of hills farther west.

Mines were often in hills, weren't they? Not on the open plain.

He continued west.

And Jessie and Ki shadowed him from far back. Did he know where he was going?

When he came to the low hills, Elsby studied them and the ground. There were no tracks, but the ground seemed to encourage travel in one direction and not in the other. He followed the path of least resistance.

There were a lot of hills; it would take time to poke around all of them, but as long as he was here . . .

He made camp and decided to move out on horseback each day to investigate. A methodical man, he started first in the north and spent three days riding in and around the hills, gradually working his way south.

He came at last into a narrow valley that opened out to a flat area. Elsby sat his horse and smiled at the mine holes in the steep-sided hills. Was this the place?

Someone had been here in the near past and had chopped up one of the old tumbledown shacks for firewood. Of course it could have been a wandering prospector or any drifter passing through.

He went back for the buckboard and drove it to the mine area. Then he started investigating the mine holes.

★

Chapter 23

Joel Dewey served his three-month term and was turned out of the Farrington jail and told to leave town. His horse had been impounded and was returned to him, and a deputy went along to see he bought victuals and took the road south.

"Don't come back."

Joel hacked his beard off with a knife till it was only several inches long. He would buy a razor the first chance he got.

He left the road and went south and west and came at last to Alister, where he and Vigil had stayed once. He got a bath and a shave and began to feel more human. He saw no posters with his picture on them—other posters had taken their place. Three months was a long time, after all. The law had moved on.

He got a job swamping out a saloon; it paid very little, but enough to live on—barely. The job included sweeping out the upstairs whores' cubicles, which he didn't mind at all. It was fun bantering with the girls. He hadn't even seen a female for three months.

He was young and not bad-looking, so the girls kidded him and teased him. They soon discovered they could tease him into an erection that poked his pants out. It became a favorite game . . .

Joel had not had a drink or a sip of beer for three months either. The second day he was on the job, he spent too much on whiskey at the end of the day, and one of the girls came to sit with him and bandy words. It was fun to get the kid drunk, and it didn't take much.

The girl called herself Alice. Her name changed often, but that week it was Alice. She had read it somewhere. "What's your name, honey?"

"Joe . . . Joel . . ."

"Joseph?"

He was fuzzy, but he knew he shouldn't tell anyone his name. Joseph was good enough. He smiled at her and nodded.

She asked, "Where you come from?"

"Didn' come from nowhere."

"Ever'body's gotta come from somewhere."

"I didn'." He downed the whiskey in front of him. He had come from somewhere, but he couldn't remember . . . He peered at her, seeing several images, foggy and blurry.

She was talking about money. He didn't get the gist of it, but he heard the word money.

"I—I'm rich," he said. "Rich's hell." He began to giggle.

She didn't believe him, of course. "Come on, you're *poor* as hell. What you workin' in here for if you's rich?"

He waggled a finger at her. "I got money . . . s' out there, hid. Got it hid . . ."

"Yeah, sure you have."

"I have . . ."

She laughed and got up. At the bar she had a sip of beer with Charlie, the bartender. "The kid over here, says he's rich."

"What you mean, rich?"

"Says he's got money hid."

Charlie looked at the kid. "He's drunk."

"Yeah." She went upstairs.

Joel staggered up after a bit and tottered to the door and out. Charlie watched him go. The things drunks got into their heads . . .

But during the evening Charlie listened to a conversation two men were having across the bar from him. The bank money had never been found, a million dollars of it, still hidden somewhere.

It was the word "hidden" that interested him. Alice had said the kid had money hid.

He thought about it that night when he went home to his room. In the morning, he drifted to the local deputy's office and asked about the bank robbery.

The deputy asked, "You know something, friend?"

"Naw. I hear about it in the saloon is all. Is there a reward?"

"It's up to six thousand now."

"Do they know who done it?"

"Yeah. Man named Joel Dewey is who they looking for."

"Thanks."

He went back and talked to Alice when she got up that afternoon. "What was the kid's name?"

"What kid?"

"The one who said he was rich."

"Oh, him." She frowned. "Think it was Joe."

He patted her butt. "Thanks."

Joel didn't come to work that day. He was home in bed with the worst headache he'd ever had. Three months had been too long to go without a drink, and he'd made a pig of himself.

He pried himself out of bed late in the day, hungry as a wolf. He was still a bit dizzy, but the headache was going.

178

He opened the door and went into the rooming-house hall. Someone was talking in the kitchen, asking about him!

"You got somebody here named Joel?"

The landlady said, no, she hadn't.

Joel slipped back into his room. He had given his name as Bill Waite. Jesus! The law was still after him. He lay on the bunk and stared at the ceiling. He had better slide out when it got good and dark. They might have a picture of him that someone would recognize.

Ben Elsby poked into each of the mine holes with his pick and shovel, making sure there was no concealed hole. But he found nothing. The weeds, since the recent rains, had grown up about each hole thick and green so he had to cut them away first.

There was nothing that he thought could be considered a mine shaft—a mine shaft was a deep hole, wasn't it? But maybe Virgil didn't know what a mine shaft was and had used the word . . . Maybe.

He chopped up the rest of the weathered shack for firewood, and used up his supplies. There was nothing here. He was positive. He had looked into each of the mine holes.

He was in the wrong place. Probably too far west. He packed up and left it behind.

Jessie and Ki watched him go. He hadn't really known a thing. "He was guessing every inch of the way," Ki said. "We've wasted a week."

"But he thought it was in a mine. So maybe it is. This is just the wrong spot."

Ki nodded. "That sounds like sense. We were thinking the same thing a while back . . ."

"But how many old mines are there in this country? Not very many, I'd guess."

"They say that gold is where you find it. So a mine will

be where we find it. How do you like my philosophy?"

She sighed. "Very profound."

Joel rode out near midnight and took the road north toward Farrington. At least five months had passed since they'd hidden the money. The wanted posters on himself and on Floyd were either torn down or covered by new ones. It was time to get the treasure and hightail it.

He needed a buckboard and a shovel, and the place to steal them was Farrington. Only this time he would evade the law.

He stayed out in the sticks till long after dark, then walked his horse around the outskirts, looking for an unattended wagon. He found three in the yard of an open-air market. There was a barn nearby, and when he went close, a man got up from a chair inside the door and asked his business.

Joel said, "I'm looking for Henry."

"There ain't no Henry here."

"You alone?" Joel pretended surprise.

"Yes . . ."

Joel hit him alongside the head with the barrel of his pistol. The man collapsed, and Joel got down and dragged him inside, found some rope and tied him securely.

Then he found a pick and shovel and put them in one of the wagons, took some harness off the wall and hooked up one of the mules in the corral. He tied his horse on behind the buckboard and drove out of town, heading west.

He drove steadily west for three days, bending slightly north. For a long time he had been going over his and Virgil's movements that fateful day, recalling everything they'd done and said. Jesus, he'd had three months to think about it.

He was sure now that they had gone far, far west into some low hills. It might take a while, but he was sure he could find the place—if he didn't give up too easily. Those mine holes in the hillsides would be there for decades. All he had to do was find them.

On the fourth day out he thought he saw two distant figures, but when he halted the wagon and stood to get a better view, they were gone. Maybe he'd been mistaken . . .

He came at last to a jumble of hills and camped in a shallow valley. They looked very much like the hills he remembered from the day with Virgil. Where should he begin? There was no point in looking for wheel ruts; the rains would have washed them all out.

But the next day, as he was riding into a grassy canyon, he came across fresh wheel marks! Someone had been here very recently with a light wagon!

He stared at the ground, swearing . . . . Then he followed the ruts, pulling his pistol to examine the loads. He rode with the Winchester across his thighs. If someone had found the cache . . . !

The tracks led into a narrow little valley that opened out to a flat area—and there were the mine holes! It was all exactly as he remembered! The visitor, whoever he had been, had chopped up most of the shack for firewood, but he had not found the secret!

It was still intact, grown over with weeds, but intact. He was a millionaire!

He got the pick and shovel out of the buckboard and began digging into the mine hole they had caved in. It looked now like the rest of the hillside.

He worked all the rest of the day. There was a huge amount of dirt to move. When he halted at dusk, he had only dug about halfway into the hole.

Jessica and Ki spotted the distant buckboard and quickly concealed themselves—hoping the owner had not seen

181

them. Was he a drifter or was it Joel Dewey on his way to the treasure?

They let Ben Elsby go on his way and turned to follow the buckboard. Ki, gazing through the binocs, described the distant traveler. "Is it Joel Dewey?" he asked.

"If so, where has he been?"

"Hiding out."

"Then he's a lot smarter than everyone gave him credit for."

Ki shrugged. "Does it take brains to hibernate?"

"Let's see if it *is* Joel Dewey."

He was easier to follow than Elsby had been. He never seemed curious about his backtrail. When he camped that night his fire was too big.

Ki was able to crawl very close and get a good look at him. It was Joel, no doubt about it. He had bought Joel drinks one time—he would not forget that face.

When he went back to Jessie, she said, "So he's come for the money. We'll let him dig it up, then take him back to Farrington."

"He'll put up a fight."

"Don't kill him. We want to hear his side of all this."

Ki nodded. "We'll do what we have to do."

The next day they watched from hiding as Joel dug farther into the mine hole. It took him the rest of the day to clear out the hole and get to the boxes.

Then he drove the buckboard close and struggled to lug the boxes out and put them aboard. It was almost dark by the time he finished.

Joel was asleep when they walked into his camp. Jessie built up the fire as Ki slipped Joel's pistol and rifle away, then nudged the sleeper.

Joel woke with a start, grabbing for the missing pistol. Ki

showed him the muzzle of the Colt. "Settle down, Joel."

He glared at them. "Who are you?"

"We've come to take you in."

Joel sank back, staring at them. Then he began to cry.

Watch for

LONE STAR AND THE CHEYENNE SHOWDOWN

100th novel in the exciting LONE STAR series
from Jove

Coming in December!

WESTERNS!

at least a savings of $3.00 each month below the publishers price. Second, there is never any shipping, handling or other hidden charges—Free home delivery. What's more there is no minimum number of books you must buy, you may return any selection for full credit and you can cancel your subscription at any time. A TRUE VALUE!

Mail the coupon below

To start your subscription and receive 2 FREE WESTERNS, fill out the coupon below and mail it today. We'll send your first shipment which includes 2 FREE BOOKS as soon as we receive it.

From the Creators of Longarm!

Featuring the beautiful Jessica Starbuck and her loyal half-American half-Japanese martial arts sidekick Ki.